She related her memories of the morning to her uncle over dinner, who occasionally punctuated her narrative with the comment, "wasn't that a bit risky?" Later, she took them to bed with her, welcoming other images to fill her mind and charge her imagination—until a shrill whistle scattered them like children from a playground.

Again, the murmur of male voices, this time closer at hand, prodded her from bed and to the window…to a vision of blackened space.

What were they doing back there? The same impulse which led her to seek out a rare book in the farthest corner of a used bookstore, now propelled her to find out what business the militia had so near her uncle's property.

She shed her nightshirt and slipped into jeans, sweatshirt, and sneakers, and then into the cool night. Buster greeted her, but she confined the animal to the cabin, fearing its blithe manner not in keeping with her stealth intentions, foolhardy though they may be.

Still, once outside, the murmurs seemed distant enough that she felt like she could risk a closer look without endangering herself.

Dear Reader,

Ever wish you could spin a globe, point to a spot, and move there? Start over fresh? Well that's just what Billie Stark does...almost. Until dark undercurrents in this quiet, country hometown get just a bit out of hand, Billie is on a mission to find her way in the world alone.

Echelon Press is proud to present to you this very special offering—*Drums Along the Jacks Fork* by Henry Hoffman. This story of a woman's journey down a new path following her parents' death also explores intriguing questions of technology versus tradition, the clash of social cultures in relationships, and a bit of insight into the militia movement. It's a heartwarming story with a touch of intrigue.

We hope you will explore more offerings from Echelon, from our Elite line of mainstream fiction, as well as our lines dedicated to mystery, romance, science fiction and fantasy, thrillers, and young adult. Please check out the website at www.EchelonPress.com for our full catalogue as well as author information, our online selection of Dollar Downloads and Notable Novellas, and contests and promotions. As enticement, we've included the preview of an exciting upcoming summer release from our suspense line at the back of this book.

At Echelon we are committed to excellence in publishing and a completely enthralling reader experience. We welcome your comments and suggestions.

Enjoy!

Susan P. Sipal
Senior Editor
Echelon Press

Also available from Echelon Press and

Henry Hoffman

ENDURING EVIL

Notable Novella

www.echelonpress.com

Henry Hoffman

Drums Along
the
Jacks Fork

Echelon Press

Echelon Press
56 Sawyer Circle #354
Memphis, TN 38103

Copyright © 2004 by W.H. Hoffman
ISBN: 1-59080-308-6
www.echelonpress.com

Cover Art © 2004 Nathalie Moore
Photographer © Kelly Goshcoff

First Echelon Press paperback printing: April 2004
Elite and all its logos are trademarks of Echelon Press.

Printed in LaVergne, TN, USA

To the class of '52, SFX Elementary School

I never knew so young a body with so old a head.

William Shakespeare,
The Merchant of Venice

Prologue

It began as an innocent diversion, her interest in maps. A practical woman, she often found herself surprised by the romantic notions stirred within her by the simple sight of a road atlas. She came to love the browsing of them, a fascination whose origins traced back to the seventh grade, when her teacher introduced them as part of a class social studies project.

"Every place has its distinctive characteristics," Miss Corcoran would instruct. "That is the purpose of a map, to communicate to us the basic physical and human features that give a place meaning and character."

Beyond her teacher's vision, they also came to represent for her the possibility of adventure, the opportunity for a new and exciting life experience. It was not that her previous experiences lacked cultural accomplishment or insight, but rather that the nomad ensconced within her never seemed to be satisfied.

Nor, if the time came, would it be a matter of running from, but of running to, the chance for fulfillment that surely rested in a location she had yet to explore. When fate finally intervened, she often would carefully slide the tip of her forefinger across the surface of an opened map to the place she could only hope would possess the right combination of physical and historical factors representing the promise of a better life.

However, the years since proved otherwise, for the town

she once had committed to and settled in no longer appeared on the map. No Woodland Hills, Missouri marked her map, or any other–no place by that name to land her finger on, no in-point to verify its existence.

How does someone determine the death of a town? She wished she could ask her old teacher. Does some government body issue an official death certificate? What exactly does it take to wipe a town off the map?

Dismayed, she could only console herself with the importance of intent, for never was it her purpose to play a role in the events leading to the town's destruction.

Chapter One

March 1993

"Welcome to the Missouri Ozarks, Miss Wilhelmina Staley, and congratulations on your appointment as director of the Woodland Hills Public Library."

"Thank you." Billie sat straight and tall, with pen and pad clasped tightly in hand, eagerly awaiting her marching orders.

The man with the ruddy complexion, ample stomach, and protruding blue eyes sitting across the table from her leaned forward in his chair to tuck the tail of his unruly corduroy shirt back into his denim trousers. He looked more like a general store proprietor than a mayor, she concluded, though in fact he was both. At the moment he was trying mightily to play the role of the latter.

"An unusual first name," he said, drumming his fingers on the table now that his shirt was in its proper place. "I meant to ask you about it at the interview."

"It's the feminine form of Wilhelm. Most people call me Billie."

"Wilhelmina-Wilhelm-William-Billie–makes sense to me. And please, call me Jake. I don't think anyone in these parts would ever think of calling me Mr. Keating, except maybe my son."

She managed a smile, willing to forgive him for his preoccupation with names.

"Now, I wanted to take a few minutes to go over with you some of the items we discussed at your job interview, particularly the challenges that await you–excuse me just a

3

moment, I need to shut this thing off."

From a television set mounted on a stand stuck in the corner of the library's meeting room emanated the low chatter of news reporters. On the monitor, a tank stormed a large compound engulfed in flames. The words "Waco, Texas" scrolled across the screen. The mayor apparently had been catching up on current events while awaiting her arrival.

"Crazies all over the place," he said, reclaiming his seat. "Now, Billie, you are going to have some big shoes to fill. To most folks around here, Hodding Whitington was known as the 'The Prince of Librarians.' How they could think that, I don't know, since he was the only librarian we've ever had or most of them had ever seen. Still, I have to agree ol' Hodding was almost an institution in these parts. His passing certainly marked the end of an era for us."

She glanced at a large framed oil portrait of Mr. Whitington mounted on wall. *Now that's what a mayor should look like.*

"Mr. Whitington was not only our librarian, but a great benefactor as well. He left us a substantial amount of money from his own personal estate to continue operating his baby for years to come."

Keating reached into his shirt pocket, pulled out a crumpled piece of paper, and began to peruse it, as he continued with his briefing. "He did, however, attach one major stipulation to the allotment of funds and it is the one we alluded to at the interview."

"The matter of computers," she said.

"Yes, Mr. Whitington came from the old school. He basically believed a library should be comprised of books, a card catalog, and an attractive structure to house them. And that's the way he wanted it to remain."

He dropped the paper and steepled his fingers. "Well, that may be all well and good for the residents of Woodland Hills, but for officials from the state library and county government, it apparently poses some major problems. According to those folks, we're failing to meet the minimum standards of public library service by refusing to offer the necessary tools and resources that contribute to 'an informed citizenry.' That's essentially how they put it."

"So, no computers at all?" she responded, stung that the full extent of the matter had not been revealed at the interview, at which time Mr. Whitington's automation stipulation was couched in terms of "obstacles to overcome" and "burdensome logistical issues."

"It was his stated desire. Now, we're not bound to accept the money, but let's look at the hard facts. The money from the Whitington estate could last us far into the future." He leaned forward in his chair, which creaked under his weight. "We essentially could operate the library with minimal public funding, yet still provide a book collection and building that would be the envy of most libraries. Yes, there would be no computers, but most folks around here who want one already have the damn thing in their homes. What they want are books."

Keating settled deep into his mayor's role, arguing public policy as if addressing a town-hall gathering. "I'd be the first to tell you, Billie, Woodland Hills is neither a city nor a town. Someone once described Centerville, our little neighbor down the road, as a place with eighty people and a whole lot of hogs. I like to think of us as a place of eight hundred people and a lot less hogs. That's how we measure progress around here, by the number of hogs per capita."

She wondered if anyone in the region had ever considered

measuring progress by books per capita.

"We're more like a village, which is why folks in these parts view the library as more of a community center than an information center. Anyway, I shouldn't be telling you what a public library is. That's why we hired you here, to provide some direction to this little ship."

She was tempted to say it was unlikely to be in a forward direction, given the condition placed on her. Yet, as the mayor intimated, the provision remained in play.

"How long do we have before a decision is required as to whether we accept this condition?" She tapped her heel nervously, but under the table and out of his sight.

"As a matter of fact, a representative from the state library will be stopping by tomorrow to greet and meet with you. It would be an opportune time to discuss the matter before you make your decision. Depending on his timetable, the recommendation could be due to me within days or weeks."

He shuffled his papers into a folder and leaned back in his chair, as though the formal portion of his welcome was completed. "I told him to stop by the library tomorrow afternoon. That should at least give you time to settle in to your office."

"His name?"

"Chad Jenkins. Don't know much about him, except that he wants to get moving on this issue."

He pulled from his shirt pocket a railroad watch to check the time. "And speaking of getting moving, I have another appointment scheduled in fifteen minutes, so I am going to cut this short. I take it you have found a place to stay?"

"I'm staying with my uncle."

"Would that by chance be Ray Staley?"

"Yes, he has a guest cabin he's letting me use." Saying it

made her feel as if she was on vacation.

"How fortunate for us that Ray decided to settle here or else we may not have had you on board. Yep, I heard you were related to Ray. I was telling my wife after the interview how much his niece resembled one of our nieces–same auburn red hair, same green eyes, even the same freckles, though I hear those things are like snowflakes, no two alike." He chuckled. "Yeah, my wife is always raving how pretty our niece is—"

He suddenly interrupted his digression, undoubtedly seeing the red stop sign flashing in her eyes.

"Well, enough of this." He rose abruptly, his chair squeaking loudly as he shoved it backward. "It's time to get back to work. If you'll just hold on here a minute, I'm going to chase down one of our library volunteers and have her show you the ropes."

When he returned, he had in tow a tall, middle-aged woman, sporting a studious face, sharp eyes, prominent cheekbones, tight lips, and dark brown hair cut to neck length. A spontaneous smile from the volunteer greatly softened the stern image.

"Billie, I would like you to meet Shirley Bennington, one of our longtime volunteers. She's going to give you the grand go-around."

"Miss Staley, nice to meet you," the volunteer said.

"Please, call me Billie."

"Well, I'm going to leave you two to your business." He shook her hand firmly. "Best of luck, Billie, and I'll be back in touch with you soon."

If she needed any kind of reminder of why she'd accepted the job in the first place, it came in the afterglow of Shirley's tour, which appeared to relax both women. Mr. Whitington may have been immersed in the past, but his taste in traditional library design and décor was nearly impeccable. The library building, originally an abandoned mill, sat perched on a high bank of the Jacks Fork River. Whitington had purchased it in the 1950s and immediately transformed it into a library.

"Whatever gave him that idea?"

"It just came to him out of the blue," Shirley said.

Constructed of red brick on a solid rock foundation, the entire two floors of the building, plus porch and basement, underwent a complete renovation. The exterior work included a replacement of the shingle roof and the waterproofing of the exterior brick walls. According to Shirley, the interior phase required steel reinforcement of the first and second floors in order to sustain the weight of the book collection and equipment. In addition, insulation, new walls, windows, electrical wiring, and a plumbing and heating system were installed.

As for the interior arrangement, the second floor had been evenly divided between a meeting room and magazine reading area, which contained a large oak reading table and chairs, a brass chandelier, and a veneer inlay clock mounted over the mantle of a stone fireplace. The highlight of the first floor was the carefully crafted wooden bookshelves, oyster white in color and crowned with molded cornices. They extended perpendicularly from the sides of the walls, their bases molded to match the baseboard.

Anchored a short distance from the front entrance sat a vintage card catalog, the wooden variety that was rapidly becoming an endangered species within the public library establishment. The divide between the traditional catalog and their electronic replacements had come to represent the demarcation line between past and future library practice. Only a few of the wooden kind remained, mostly in places like

Woodland Hills, where heritage was not easily dispensed with, as evidenced by Mr. Whitington's dictum. A small reading area and a custom-designed circulation desk, made of maple, fronted the librarian's office and staff workroom, completing the first floor layout.

"Well, Billie, that's about it," her guide said, as they stood on the steps of the building's porch at the conclusion of the tour. "I understand your first full day on the job is tomorrow. I wish you the best of luck. I'm sure if Mr. Whitington were still with us, he would be pleased we found someone to carry on his work. If you think of any questions in the meantime, let me know and I'll try and answer them."

A sincere smile creased the volunteer's face.

"Thanks, Shirley," Billie replied politely, shaking the woman's hand. A feeling of relief came to her, as she felt a professional connection with the volunteer.

As she descended the porch steps, she paused to gaze down First Street, the road that led from the library to State Road 80, the main highway intersecting the town only four blocks away. The juncture of the two roads formed what could be defined as the city's center, comprised of the Keating General Store, which also housed the mayor's office, a post office, a feed store, a two-pump filling station, an auto repair garage, and a café. Somewhere near the intersection was a sign that read "St. Louis–220 miles." Her odometer had registered 205 miles when she'd driven it.

Whichever, she had come a long way, to a place where the bark of a dog or the crow of a rooster pierced the air with far more frequency than the roar of an engine or the cry of a child. Two prior visits to her uncle's place had led her to conclude that the town had no vision of becoming a tourist mecca, like its neighbor to the west, Branson.

There obviously was no grand plan to enhance its scenic setting by altering the natural formation of the encompassing terrain. Even the most earnest of environmentalists would find no evidence of wanton grading and cutting into greenly forested hillsides or the cutting off of gently sloping hilltops in order to plant a building at the highest point, as if to announce the town's arrival or grant it stature. Nor was there a residue of unsightly outdoor advertising, derelict buildings, junkyards, or wrecking lots.

No, there were no extraordinary enhancements nor degradations to be seen. The residents of Woodland Hills apparently sought neither the grand nor the spectacular, nor the quaint or the picturesque. They obviously preferred a gently bucolic scene, which at least on the surface evoked a sense of tranquility and peace.

As she looked about, a sense of home filled her. Drawing a deep breath, she continued on her way.

She crossed a washboard gravel parking lot to a dirt path road leading to her uncle's house less than a mile away. The path paralleled the Jacks Fork, allowing passersby a close-up view of the softly gurgling stream as it coiled its way through acres of tree-lined hills on its journey south.

Halfway home she spotted a large boulder partially imbedded in the river's bank. Impulsively, she scaled the rock's smooth surface to gain an unobstructed view of the stream's downward flow. She gazed at its still surface and the clear reflection of surrounding trees, many of whose limbs arced over the water's edge, as though poised to drink from the enticing offering below.

Her reverie lasted but a few moments, as a sudden gust of cool wind wafted down the hillsides carrying with it a reminder of another hillside setting and a tragedy that ultimately led her to the path she presently was traveling. She hugged her arms across her chest, as if fending off a chill.

It was on the eastern slope of the Rockies, not far from Colorado Springs, where a search party had found her parents' downed private plane. Their small prop job had been no match for the steep slopes turned even more treacherous by a sudden thunderstorm.

Until the aftermath of that day, she'd never given much thought to being an only child. Oh, occasionally, she would come across an article analyzing those afflicted with the syndrome, how they were lavished with attention and spared disciplinary measures to the point of becoming irreparably spoiled.

She paid little heed to the arguments. She gave her parents greater credit than did many of the experts. Because of them she felt normal by most social standards. Having them taken away in such a sudden manner caused her not only great grief, but a long pause to reexamine her goals in life.

Her parents had been rare book dealers, an occupation she had also embraced after joining them in the business at age twenty, following her graduation from college. She was known in the trade as a "book scout," one who monitors book catalogs, book sales, book fairs, and auctions for first editions and reader's copies. She was responsible for tracking the fluctuation in bibliographic value.

What began as a curiosity for her parents about the worth of a box of dusty volumes uncovered in a friend's attic blossomed into a profitable hobby and then eventually into a living for the family. She had become their partner, in addition to being their only child. Upon their deaths she soon realized that it wasn't the business, but the books that held her interest. So, reluctantly, she had sold the enterprise to another dealer, and with the profits paid her way through library science graduate school. She was no longer an antiquarian, but a librarian, though Mr. Whitington from his grave might soon think otherwise.

With a last glance at the river and deep indrawn breath, she abandoned her perch atop the rock. Her steps swift and determined, she resumed her walk home, past a succession of wood-framed houses, their tidy backyards lined with hammocks slung between trees, and with outdoor grills of every design. At last, she reached a large vacant lot, beyond which rested a final house, its weathered wood panels peeking from behind worn layers of gray paint. Adjoining it was a small cabin. Two pickups, her uncle's blue Bronco and her red Ranger, both displaying their age, sat side by side on a small carport at the back of the complex. The image was a stark reminder of how far she had traveled in such a short time.

Just be thankful, she told herself upon arrival, that you have a house to come home to and an uncle to remind you of a life that once was. *It's up to you to make your way now.*

"What are you watching there, Uncle Ray?" she asked as she entered her uncle's living room, though recognizing immediately the replay of the Waco incident flashing across the television set he'd stationed across from his couch.

"Crazies everywhere," he replied in a manner that invited a further probe on her part.

"That's what the mayor said, so it must mean you have them in these parts, right?"

"We have our share, Billie, and stuff like this is likely to stir them up even more." He nodded to the screen

"How do you mean?"

"The militia people. They've been beating their drums

around here, too. They think the federal government is out to get us, just like they're getting Waco."

At the moment, the federal government and militia movement seemed far removed from her. "And they're active here? I thought Michigan was their state of choice."

"Like I said, we have our share."

"But not you."

"Nah, Billie, I'm finished fighting battles, not to say that is a worthy one to begin with. Hell, I've done enough fighting *for* the federal government, why would I want to fight against it?"

She recalled her father's occasional references to his brother's battlefield exploits in Korea, his Purple Heart, and his reluctance to talk about it.

"Have they tried to recruit you?"

"They came to do a little fishin', but like I told them, the bait doesn't exist for me to bite on."

She smiled with pride. "They need to learn how to fish like you do, Uncle Ray."

She patted him on the shoulder and then joined him on the couch.

"How'd your first day go?" he asked, as he clicked off the television.

"As well as could be expected, I suppose. There were a few surprises."

"Like what?"

"Like the mayor. He wore a less professional face from the one he had on at the job interview. How did he ever become mayor?"

"Around here, it's a matter of whoever wants to be mayor. I've heard say that a few people, especially women, can find him overbearin' at times."

"Let's hope that's not the case all of the time."

"Whoa there, Billie. Are you tellin' me you may be having second thoughts about this job?" He turned, studying her face, concern reflected in his blue eyes. "Maybe, I shouldn't have brought it to your attention in the first place."

"No, no." She squeezed his arm. "No need to be concerned about that, Uncle Ray. I appreciate your help. Everyone has to start somewhere, whether it's in starting a new life or new job. In my case it just happens to be both."

What she also wanted to say, but did not, was that she no longer would have her parents to serve as her safety net.

"It's too bad you didn't take time out to visit the place on one of your earlier visits here with your folks. You could have got a better feel for the operation."

"I could never have torn myself away from one of those fishing trips with you, Uncle Ray." She laughed. "Anyhow, the view is always better from the outside looking in. Now that I'm on the inside, I'll learn what needs to be done."

"How's the cabin working out?"

"Perfect. It's all I need for now." A simple place to start over, to heal as she chartered this new course in her life.

Her uncle slumped back in his seat, as if relieved. "Is Buster a bother? Sometimes he gets to chasing coons late at night."

"No, he's good company. Did I tell you I had a retriever once, a chocolate lab, just like Buster? He also seemed to take a great interest in my comings and goings."

"Don't be fooled; he's just lookin' for a handout. And speaking of that, how about if I fixed a couple of chicken salad sandwiches for us?"

"Sounds good."

They lunched on a tiny backyard patio framed by ivy-covered lattices. A large, freshly seeded vegetable garden fronting the area was all that separated them from her cabin home across the way. The patio and garden were where her uncle chose to spend most of his waking hours, tilling the garden during the day and listening to nature's symphony in the evening while planted in one of his lawn chairs.

She'd observed him through the cabin's kitchen window the night before. For a long period he'd sat virtually motionless, as if etched into the surrounding scenery. There was a hint of her father in him, an easy manner that allowed him to carry his large frame, broad chest, and square shoulders in a quiet yet imposing manner. Though he appeared a bit rougher around the edges than did her father, his haggard face, combined with his grizzled mane and gravelly voice, projected the image of a man confident of himself and his surroundings. He seemed a settled man, but unlike her father, he'd never married, for whatever reasons that were his own.

Still, the resemblance to her father comforted her. As if the connection could never be truly broken as long as the memory of him remained alive within her.

It must have been an hour into his evening ritual before she noticed any movement from him that first night, an opening of the eyes precipitated by the distant sound of a train whistle. It was one of the many freight trains headed south out of St. Louis and now making its long loop around Woodland Hills. That much she'd already learned from him. He certainly would have known, having spent his entire working life as a switchman for the Missouri Pacific Railroad.

Instinctively, he had retrieved the railroad watch he carried in his overalls to check the time. At the same moment, she realized that to her uncle the cry of the whistle was as much a call to the wild as the other howls that filled the nighttime air.

"Before you leave, I have something for you," he said,

15

returning her to the present, as they finished off their sandwiches. "FedEx delivered it this morning."

"Oh, what is it?" Like a child, her heart lifted with the promise of a treat.

She watched him amble back inside and in a few moments return with a metal briefcase.

He hesitated briefly, as if not sure what to say. Then, "Not long ago, Billie, I got a call from one of the FAA people who was assigned to investigate your parents' plane crash. He told me this had been discovered several miles from the crash zone long after their final report had been filed."

"How did it get there—that far from the crash site?"

"I asked the same thing. He didn't know. Said that sometimes debris from accidents could turn up in the strangest of places. As you can see, it has a few bumps and bruises, but for the most part it came through in one piece."

He watched her intently, evidently trying to judge her reaction to the unexpected voice from the past.

She took the briefcase and upon opening it discovered inside a padded package with the words, "To Billie," scribbled on its front side. Her father's handwriting.

The words struck quickly, opening an old wound with the precision of a skilled surgeon's scalpel.

"He also said there was a possibility it could have been thrown from the plane. That sometimes happens, especially in light plane crashes."

Her heart thumped loudly in her ears. "Thrown by the plane or thrown by *them*?"

"I don't know." He shook his head slowly, his eyes widened. "I should have asked."

She paused at the notion and then proceeded to open the package. Inside she discovered an item she recognized immediately, a copy of Anna Sewell's *Black Beauty*, a first edition, and in surprisingly excellent condition. She took a deep breath and then slowly ran the tips of her fingers across the book's smooth binding.

"Somethin' special?" her uncle asked.

"Very special," she whispered.

"I have a feelin' there is more to that book than meets the eye."

"Yes, you're right, Uncle Ray."

He harrumphed, as if loosening tightness in his throat. "Well, I have some chores to do, so I am going to leave you alone with your thoughts."

"And I need to finish my unpacking," she replied, inserting the book back into the pouch and briefcase, before returning to the cabin.

To her home alone, to wallow in the memories of her parents' love and the balm of their parting gift.

While completing her unpacking, she had time to take full measure of her new living quarters. Outside the cabin, a veranda ran the full length of the dwelling and included a grill and chain-suspended porch swing. Inside, consisted of a mini-kitchen, a single bedroom, and a bunk bed. A combination dining and living room included a desk where she placed her personal computer, a wood-burning stove, and a rusted window air conditioner. A half bath with an old porcelain tub and shower, and several space heaters strategically located throughout the unit, completed the arrangement.

It certainly wasn't the lifestyle she'd grown accustomed to and it would take some adjustment. However, by the time she scattered about her personal belongs and mementos, the place took on the appearance of a home, if only a temporary one.

She saved her most difficult chore for last, that of fitting her limited wardrobe into a more limited bedroom closet. It appeared to be a hunter's closet, designed for those items that could not be tossed onto the porch alongside the wet parkas and fishing boots. As her final act, she arranged a week's worth of work clothing, combinations that would somehow reflect a transition from casual chic to casual country, if indeed that was the proper designation.

Later that evening, her tasks complete, she lay on her bed reviewing recent library documents, including budgets, which might provide her some background information for future decisions. The day, however, had taken its toll and she soon drifted into a half-sleep, the anticipations of the day and days to come having been calmed by the soothing cadences of the hills drifting through an open bedroom window.

The plaintive wail of a freight train was the last sound she recalled hearing before being awakened by another whistle, not a distant one, nor a lonesome one, but one accompanied by raised male voices, large numbers of them, coming from the woods.

Startled, she checked the clock on a nearby nightstand. Two hours had passed since she'd fallen asleep.

Billie rose from her bed and glanced out the window, but saw nothing, her vision tarred by the pitch of the night. Sensing no movement nearby, she slipped out her front door and onto the veranda where she could broaden her view. Again, she detected no movement, except for Buster who trotted into sight, his tail in full swing. The thought of waking her uncle came to mind, but quickly faded. If Buster wasn't concerned, neither was she.

Still, she invited the pet in to spend the night with her...just in case.

Chapter Two

"Yep. It's the militia folk," Uncle Ray replied between sips of morning coffee.

"How long have they been meeting in the woods back there?" Billie studied her uncle's face.

He wrinkled his brow. "Some time now."

"Buster didn't seem overly concerned."

"That's because he's used to it."

"I have to say; I found it a bit disconcerting." She kept her tone deliberately calm, conscious of her uncle peering intently at her over the rim of his coffee cup.

"Don't worry, Billie. They have no quarrel with you."

"But they do with you?" she asked.

He shrugged.

"But they don't with me, you say."

"I can't imagine what that could be." He dropped his mug on the table top with a thud. "You travelin' by foot this morning?"

Apparently, he didn't want to talk about the militia.

"No. I need to cart some boxes of materials to work, so I'm taking the truck."

"Need a hand with the boxes?"

"Sure."

They loaded her truck and then exchanged a warm hug.

"Uncle Ray, you would have made a good father," she proclaimed, climbing into the cab.

"Yeah, maybe so," he replied with a winsome smile, as

though the thought had crossed his mind as regularly and as distant as the call of a train echoing through the night.

With Shirley lending a hand, Billie was able in good time to unload and unpack the boxes, file the papers, store the supplies, and arrange her office in a style that she hoped both the public and staff would find accommodating.

She was down to her last unpacked box when she asked, "That empty corner bookcase you showed me on the second floor during the tour, did the library have something planned for it?"

"No. Mr. Whitington purchased it at an antique store shortly before his death. We had no idea what he intended for it."

"I think I'm about to make my first executive decision. Come, follow me." She grabbed the remaining box and headed for the second floor with her volunteer in tow.

"Is there a key for this?" Billie asked, upon reaching the bookcase.

"Yes, but we've kept it unlocked, since there is nothing of value inside."

"Maybe we can remedy that," she mused, soaking in the elegance of the furnishing.

The spoon carved oak bookcase easily exceeded her five and a half-foot frame. Its twin doors featured decorative key locks, brass pulls, and glass panels that permitted a clear view of the adjustable wooden shelves inside. She'd seen this style of bookcase while on her book scouting sojourns. The Louis XV styles were popular in France where older, aristocratically designed homes, boasting high ceilings and windows, invited tall items of furniture.

Spurred by a rush of enthusiasm, she opened wide the two

doors and removed *Black Beauty* from its container.

"Wow, how old is that?" Shirley asked, the enthusiasm in her voice underscoring their shared interest in classic literature.

"It's a first American edition, close to a century old," Billie said reverently as she aligned it on one of the middle shelves.

"Where did you get it?"

"My parents obtained it on their last book auction trip."

Satisfied with its positioning, she proceeded to add another book to the adjoining case, a first edition of Robert Louis Stevenson's *Treasure Island*.

"Was that also a gift from your parents?"

"No. This one I tracked down on my own. I decided to hang on to it as a reminder of my previous vocation."

Billie gently closed the doors and took a step back to admire the view. "Well, what do you think, Shirley? Would Mr. Whitington have had any objections?"

"I think not," she replied, "but I do think you had better grab a bite to eat. That state library representative is due in your office in less than an hour."

Shirley was ever the practical one, Billie was beginning to learn.

She took one more glance at the display. It was a first step, maybe even the beginning of a bonding with her new setting. Breathing a note of expectation, she turned the lock on that thought, and headed back to her office.

Billie had just tossed her empty lunch bag into the trash, when an earnest-looking man wearing a blue shirt, red tie, and official smile tapped on her opened office door.

"Ms. Staley? Chad Jenkins."

"Yes—I've been expecting you Mr. Jenkins." She rose in greeting. "Won't you have a seat?"

He appeared to be in his mid-forties, though a full beard and shaved head made it difficult to determine.

"Congratulations on your appointment. I understand from the mayor this is your first day on the job," he said, maintaining his smile.

"Yes, and from what he's told me, there is an item or two you would like to discuss with me," she replied, wiping the smile from his face.

"Well, I guess we might as well get right down to business." He sat in the chair opposite her desk and opened his briefcase. "As I'm sure you know, the immediate issue on the table concerns a decision made by your predecessor, one we at the state library are hoping you might reconsider."

"Automation."

"Yes. To be blunt, Mr. Whitington's position, if it remains as is, could lead to a cutoff of state funding for your library. It also places in jeopardy the benefits you derive from full participation in the state's development of regional library systems and inter-library cooperative efforts."

"Like inter-library loans, etc." She wondered if he'd been as blunt to Mr. Whitington as he was to her.

"And universal borrowing privileges, and the many staff development services, and collection development programs sponsored by the state library." He looked up from the papers he was rifling through. "You might be interested in knowing that Mr. Whitington, in a rare moment of candor, once confessed to us his desire for the public library to be preserved in its natural state."

"Interesting concept. *This* public library or all of them?"

"We didn't ask, but unless you're looking to be considered the little library that roared, Ms. Staley, it could prove to be embarrassing, especially to a professional in the field like you.

If you're not the last remaining public library in the state holding on to one of those traditional card catalogs planted outside your office, you're close to the last."

She listened politely, as he sought to close the sale, but she wasn't quite ready to buy. Oh, she understood the stakes well enough, and she was all for progress, but the issue was not so simple.

"Granted, it might be the kind of human-interest story media from around the country might take an interest in. It could even give the city a notoriety it might otherwise never achieve. I did read once that every small town is entitled to one big event in its lifetime." He paused, grinning. "This could be it for Woodland Hills. Nevertheless, I think you are aware of what's at risk."

"Yes, I am aware."

Images flickered in her mind of newspaper cartoons depicting her in various states of battle dress, as she gallantly stood guard over the card catalog.

"Let me ask you something, Mr. Jenkins. You speak of the disadvantages to us. I would be interested in hearing what you consider to be the advantages of Mr. Whitington's position."

"Advantages?"

"Yes. I've always believed that what elevates a matter to the status of an issue, which obviously this has become, is the recognition of two sides to it. You mentioned this as the immediate issue on the table, so I'm assuming you acknowledge there is another side."

He flushed slightly. "Look, Ms. Staley, I'm not here to argue the book versus the computer. Personally, I believe the two can co-exist. I do, however, represent a state agency whose mission it is to quote 'promote libraries throughout the state in order to enrich the quality of life for the people of Missouri.' That's my job."

"Just a moment," she said, politely raising the finger of one hand while shuffling through some papers on her desk with the other, until she settled on one. "This is from the most recent annual report of our library. It says here 'it is the mission of the Woodland Hills Public Library to enrich the quality of life for the people of the community.' That's my job, Mr. Jenkins, and there's the rub. My first responsibility is to the local community, and yours is to the state."

"I think Mr. Whitington, when he used our mission statement as a model, conveniently left out the part about providing the public full access to information. If you continue to travel your present course, what you will end up with is a library where what you see is what you get, and little more."

She shifted in her chair at the last thought. "Perhaps so, and I'm not saying you are wrong in your judgment. In fact, you may well be right. I realize the computer is breaking down not only library walls but also library definitions. Does this mean this library, lacking a computer, no longer qualifies as a library? I assume you've had a chance to see it, Mr. Jenkins. What would you call it?"

"I would call it a private library, one that I would love to have in my house, except it's bigger than my house." He smiled with not a little bit of charm, drawing his face less serious, more human. "Maybe I could have it as an annex with an ornate hallway connecting the two."

He spread his arms in a sweeping gesture to indicate the scope of his vision.

"And on which side would you place your computer?"

"Well, I would have to think about that, but let's not confuse the issue."

"I agree. I would just like to think there is still a place in the public square for a library like this one. Maybe Woodland Hills is the place. Then again, my rare book background could be clouding my view. Like I said, you may well be right and I may end up having to face that age-old question: Do I vote my conscience or my constituents?"

"You can always persuade them."

"Or they persuade me." She pushed back from her desk. They'd obviously covered all the bases and she had work to do. "When do you need a final decision?"

"In two months and no later, I'm afraid. That's according to the state librarian."

"Fine. I will let you know by then," she said, rising from her chair.

"We will look forward to hearing from you." The official smile had crept back onto his face before shaking her hand.

She watched him leave and stroll past the library stacks toward the main entrance, suddenly stopping to glance at the card catalog, as if he had spotted a nesting whooping crane.

She flipped her desk calendar to a month and a half–to the day–to note that her recommendation was coming due.

"How'd it go?" Shirley asked from the doorway.

"About as I expected. No surprises."

"Unfortunately, I have one for you."

Billie raised an eyebrow. "Oh, a big one?"

"I hate for this to happen on your fist day, but we have a problem. Some time back Mr. Whitington set up an oral history program. Three people registered for it." Shirley watched her hesitantly, as if unsure of her reaction. "The bad part is that the first session is scheduled to start in fifteen minutes. What with his death and the change of command, we completely forgot about it, Billie. Do you want us to postpone or cancel it?"

"Are they here?"

"They are waiting in the meeting room, all three of them. Do you know anything about oral history programs?"

"Enough, maybe, to get them started. Did Mr. Whitington have a program outline?"

She'd actually completed an oral history project for her graduate studies and found it quite interesting. Unexpected insight often emerged when people were allowed to tell their stories in their own words.

"Not that I am aware of," Shirley said. "We did post an announcement on the bulletin board, but it pretty much was limited to time and place. We do have the registrations, however, which asked for some background info on the participants."

"Can you get me those? And do we have a cassette recorder?"

"A computer we may not have. A recorder we do," Shirley cracked, as she left to retrieve it and the registrations.

The wary look on the faces of the two middle-aged men and older woman awaiting her at a small circular table was one she had encountered before during her brief stints as a substitute teacher. She wondered in joining them, if her own wariness was as apparent.

"Hello. My name is Billie Staley and in case you didn't know, I am the new librarian here at Woodland Hills. I also will be filling in for the man who would have been conducting this program, if not for his untimely death, Mr. Whitington."

"That old fart?" the larger of the two men barked.

"Yes, Mr. Whitington," she calmly repeated. "Did he by chance provide you with any information on the program?"

"He sent us this list of events that he said might help

trigger our memories, things like the birth of a sibling, a marriage, our experiences with children," the woman said. She rummaged in her oversized purse for a notepad. "He also instructed us to jot down at least fifteen highlights of our life."

"I came up with fifty-three," said the larger man, winking at her.

"Fine. Did he explain to you the purpose of the program?"

"Not really," the woman said, shooting an exasperated look at the man who'd just interrupted her, "other than he was looking for people from this area to tell the story of their lives."

"Well, that might be a good starting point, to go over the purpose, but first let's do some introductions. You are—" she asked, nodding to Mr. Whitington's detractor.

"Ted Stark."

Billie performed a quick mental assessment: Large frame, long face, dull blue eyes, straight nose, pointed ears, silky strands of remaining hair brushed to the nape of his neck, an impulsive, engaged demeanor.

"I see here that you are a retired businessman," she commented, checking the registrations.

"You got it. Twenty-five years pursuin' the dream."

"And you are—"

"Anita Winfield."

Chubby face, slight dimples, wide brown eyes, small mouth, soft-spoken, good-natured, proper manner.

"You state here that you were once a perfusionist."

"Yes."

"Perfuminist? What the hell is that," interjected Stark.

"I'm sure we will find out, Mr. Stark, and, by the way, I see here it is spelled p-e-r-f-u-s-i-o-n-i-s-t. And you are?" she asked, turning to the remaining member.

"Jack Hatch."

Medium build, taut face, keen green eyes, tight-lipped, lank hair, intense, detached manner, she catalogued his appearance.

"And you are a retired forest ranger, right?"

"Right." He nodded curtly, as if he were not sure why he'd bothered to come.

"Okay–the purpose of this program as I see it. For a small community like ours, this kind of event in essence allows researchers to reconstruct the daily life of the town, something that otherwise would be difficult to do for a community that has no local newspaper or any other written record of general note. As Mr. Whitington said, we want you to tell us your stories. Oral histories are, by design, autobiographical recollections."

She surveyed her audience of three, analyzing their interest and comprehension. "However, I would ask you to concentrate on those aspects of your life that have a direct connection to this community. Otherwise we will end up with a surplus of information, much of it irrelevant. It might be interesting to some folks, but it doesn't mean it connects to our purpose."

She paused to allow for questions.

"What do you plan to do with the tapes?" Stark asked.

"First, we will transcribe them, following which we will sit down and review them. Then, with your permission, we'll deposit them into the collection. So, feel free with your views, for you will have the opportunity to add or delete. And allow me to remind you that I am here to listen, not interrogate."

Anxious to get started, Billie leaned forward, slid the recorder to the center of the table, and punched the "ON" button. "Okay, Mrs. Winfield, let's start with you. Tell us your story."

"From the beginning?" She adjusted her chair closer to the table.

"From the point at which you feel the pathway of your life pointed in the direction of Woodland Hills."

"Well, let's see, I spent a good part of my early life traveling the world–Europe, Australia, Canada, while working in various medical fields, mainly as a medical assistant and respiratory assistant. When I returned to the states, I took a job as a therapist at St. Mary's Medical Center in St. Louis, where I worked for five years. It so happened that while I was there, the center started up its school of perfusion, a branch of medicine I had taken an interest in. So, I switched careers in midstream. I entered and graduated from the school and became a perfusionist. Then—"

"This is probably a good place to tell us what a perfusionist is, Mrs. Winfield," Billie said, gently tapping her on the hand.

"Sure. A perfusionist is a member of an open-heart surgical team. He or she sets up and operates the heart-lung machine that basically takes over the functions of a patient's heart and lungs during the course of an operation. In many cases the heart must be stopped and nearly emptied, so it becomes necessary to bypass the blood through a machine, which continues to pump blood around the body, while at the same time adding oxygen to it. The perfusionist's job is basically to make sure the machine is operating properly."

"Could you speak up just a little, Mrs. Winfield? I'm not sure this machine is catching what you are saying," Billie politely interjected.

"Oh...okay." Then, a little louder, "It was an exciting position to be in, one that offered a lot of challenges, as well as a great sense of satisfaction from knowing that you had a direct hand in saving lives. And we had such a great team. An open-heart surgical team is actually made up of four separate teams–the surgical team, the team of nurses, the anesthesiologists, and the perfusionists. We had terrific communication and interaction among us. We not only depended on each other but trusted each other. That was until–excuse me–this could be a little difficult to get through."

Her face had gone from enthusiasm of the job she'd obviously loved to showing signs of distress, long and drawn-out, her eyes glistening.

Billie patted her hand again, and in a soothing voice said, "Take your time, Mrs. Winfield."

"Well, there came this day, one I am condemned to live over and over, I'm afraid." She paused, gulping. "Let me see if I can explain it to you clearly. The hospital we were operating in had two nearly identical open-heart surgery rooms. We had a heart-lung machine in each room; one was an older model of the other. For some unknown technical reason, the older one had been modified in such a way that the forward and reverse switches had been interchanged. As a result, the older model's vent–that's the plastic tubing–ran in a clockwise, forward direction, while the vent in the newer model ran in a counter-clockwise, direction. I was aware of the modification. However, one day when we had a heavy caseload and we were working both rooms, I inadvertently forgot which room I was in and turned the vent on backwards."

She stopped and shook her head slowly from side to side before proceeding, a shiver shaking her. "The surgeon proceeded to insert the vent without checking it, so the machine ended up pumping air into the patient rather than sucking blood out. Once we realized what was happening, it was too late. The man died on the operating table." She ended in a choked, almost inaudible gasp.

"Oh man! That reminds me of the time I wound up in the wrong restroom of this club I used to run." Mr. Stark leaned forward, his voice enthused and rough. "Some redneck gal nearly put me six feet under with this pistol she pulled on me. I was—"

"Mr. Stark, you will have a chance to tell your story," Billie said, attempting to maintain a neutral tone. "We would like for these presentations to be more of a monologue rather than a conversation, so let's give Mrs. Winfield a chance to finish her story."

He crossed his arms over his chest. "Why are we all here at the same time then, if you don't want any feedback from us?"

"That's a very good question, Mr. Stark." Billie kept her voice deliberately neutral. She'd dealt with men like him before and refused to let him intimidate her. "I don't know what Mr. Whitington had in mind. However, I have no objection to a little feedback. It could stir some memories that otherwise might be left out. The point is to keep the story on track."

"Well, then, I would like to know what her story has to do with Woodland Hills."

"Each of your stories, when taken as a whole, Mr. Stark, become part of the fabric for the story of the community. They—"

"I'll tell him what the connection is," Mrs. Winfield interrupted with determination, fire lighting her brown eyes.

The tone in her voice prompted a raised eyebrow from Mr. Hatch, who for most of the session had been sitting with hands clasped across his midriff, his eyes fixed in space.

"The victim was a fifty-five-year-old man by the name of Stewart Benson. Do any of you recognize that name?" she asked to those assembled.

"No." "Nope." "Don't think so," came the succession of replies.

"Well, he was the son of Chester Benson." She arched a brow, a triumphant gleam in her eye. "Have you heard that name?"

Another round of negative nods heightened the curiosity.

"Long before this building was renovated," she continued, "when it was still the old mill, you would have noticed a small plaque, not far from the front entrance, honoring Mr. Benson for his work. He was the master millwright who built this building."

"How interesting, Mrs. Winfield. Did the younger Mr. Benson have family here?" Billie asked, seeking to expand the connection, her interest captured by the thrill of historical discovery.

"Yes, and that is how I ended up here. He lived with his invalid mother and took care of her every need. I learned this by doing the unusual and contacting her some time after the incident. Though I knew there was an insurance settlement, I still felt an obligation to check into her welfare, since she was the sole remaining member of the family."

A hint of pride crept into the wrinkles of concern surrounding her eyes. "I had learned during my career how important it was to treat the patient as if he or she was a member of my own family. I realized the necessity of maintaining some distance between myself as a professional employee and the patient, but most of the equipment and surroundings of a critical care unit are cold and frightening to patients and their loved ones. So, there needs to be some empathy displayed to counteract the sterile atmosphere. Anyway, she was very understanding of me and recognized the incident for what it was—an accident."

Billie expected Stark to jump in again for whatever reason, but apparently the connection made between the town and the incident served well enough to keep him quiet for the moment.

Mrs. Winfield breathed a long sigh and leaned back in her chair, obviously strained somewhat by the stress of her story. "When I asked if she would be okay, she mentioned that she probably had no choice but to enter into an assistant care facility in a larger town. It was then that an idea popped into my head. As things turned out, I did not lose my perfusionist license as a result of the accident. However, I did make the decision to leave the profession and try my hand at home nursing, a line of work I felt would put some space between me and the institutional workplace, which I was beginning to tire of."

She spread her hands wide, surveying her rapt audience. Even Jack Hatch appeared captivated. "So, I asked myself, why not set up a home nursing practice in or near Woodland Hills where I would be able to assist Mrs. Benson, enabling her to stay in her own home? At first, she seemed surprised, then interested, then accepting. So, I moved here and set up a little home nursing business, which I ran for about 20 years before retiring."

"And Mrs. Benson?"

"Mrs. Benson lived until she was ninety-two, when she died in her sleep of natural causes. She is buried next to her husband and son over at Memorial Gardens."

Billie allowed a few moments for the story to sink in and then punched the recorder's "OFF" button. A smidgen of history, but one to build on, she believed.

"I think this will do for today. Thank you, Mrs. Winfield,

for providing us with your story. We shall see you all next week, same time, same place."

"That was quick. Who goes next?" Mr. Stark chimed in.

"I have a week to consider that, and since I am one who takes all of the time allotted me before making a decision, we'll just have to wait and see," she responded with a wink.

The schedule mix-up may not have qualified as a major problem, she mused, as she walked out the door, but she had survived it.

"I swear, this is the last time I will ask you this question today. How did it go?"

Balancing an armload of books that almost covered her face, Shirley stopped before Billie, headed down the hallway returning to her office.

"Reasonably well, though I wish I had devoted a little more time for introductory chit-chat, so I could have established a better rapport before beginning. Here, let me help you with those." She removed half the stack from Shirley's strained arms. "Still, it could have been worse. By the way, do you recall a commemorative plaque that was mounted near the front entrance of this building before the renovation?"

"I can't say that I do. Who was it commemorating?" She dropped her books on the front desk.

With a sigh of relief, Billie deposited hers as well. "A man by the name of Chester Benson. He built the building."

Shirley tapped her lip in thought. "There's a storage cabinet in the basement that is stuffed with miscellaneous items left over from the old building."

"My curiosity has the best of me." She eagerly clasped Shirley's arm, nudging her along. "Let's take a look."

She trailed Shirley to the basement doorway located in the

staff workroom and down a wooden stairwell that led to a maze of boxes and furnishings stacked to the ceiling. Deftly maneuvering through the narrow passages, they worked their way to a corner metal cabinet.

"What's in all of these boxes?" Billie asked, shoving one aside with her foot.

"Books."

"Books?"

"Yes, old books, ones that Mr. Whitington could not bear to throw out. He knew the day was fast approaching when lack of space would leave him no choice, but now the choice is yours."

Billie was about to take a peek into one of the boxes, when Shirley swung open the cabinet's doors to reveal another crowded condition. Crammed onto the unit's utility shelves were piles of spiral notebooks, leftover office supplies, sundry pieces of small equipment, and signage from the old building.

As Shirley began to poke through one side of the cabinet, Billie probed through the other, until her fingers lighted upon what appeared to be a photo album lodged beneath some accounting ledgers, under that she found a plaque.

"Well, well," she said, taking it into her hands and raising it to the light, the reward of holding history in her hands running through her. She stared at the simple inscription.

Chester Benson–Master Millwright–1900.

"Look at these photos," Shirley swooned, peeling back the pages of the album.

They were mostly shots of men, women, and children, outfitted in their turn-of-the-century finery, posing for the camera in front of the mill. One of a handsome man and a young boy, decked out in straw hats and ties, sitting on an old mare. A handwritten caption beneath indicated that it was

Chester Benson and his son, Stewart.

Billie slowly passed her fingers over the photo, absorbing the aura of days gone by, pointing to a portion of it.

"Look at the supply wagon parked against the wall. Do you suppose that was Benson's private stall?"

"And do you notice the water bucket and lantern?" Shirley asked, a ripple of excitement in her voice.

"On the porch, yes."

"Let me show you something else you missed on the tour."

They retraced their steps through the congestion of boxes to a storage closet at the opposite end of the basement.

"Tell me if these look familiar," the volunteer remarked, swinging open the door.

Propped against one wall of the room was a wagon wheel and against the opposite wall, a wagon tongue. Hanging from hooks mounted on the back wall were a lantern, water bucket, bridle, and rope.

"The same items in the photo?" Billie stepped eagerly into the room to examine the items better.

"The wheel and tongue for sure, I would say. The others may have come later."

"What's the rope for? Certainly not to raise and lower the bucket." She ran her hand along the rough length of the rope. "It's too thick. There must be fifty feet of it."

"Maybe there was a hanging tree nearby," Shirley said, her eyebrows lifted.

"Sure, but it would have had to have been a very tall tree or very short guy," she said, eliciting a stern smile from her cohort.

"Wait." Shirley drummed her forefinger on her pursed lips as though remembering something important. "I recall asking my husband about that rope years ago when this stuff first came to my attention. He came and took a look at it. He's a retired high school history teacher who considers himself an authority on old west matters. He said in olden days work crews occasionally would have to unhook the horses from a wagon, unload it and lower it down steep inclines, like riverbanks, by rope. He also made a big point of saying the rope was made of all natural fibers, not like the artificial ones of today."

Billie nodded slowly, the possibilities appealing to the treasure hunter side of her personality which had so loved the book hunt. "That sounds feasible, but why did Mr. Whitington decide to hang on to these items?"

"I believe at one time he was considering turning the basement into a historical museum."

"Mr. Jenkins from the State Library would say that Mr. Whitington already had a museum upstairs."

"Right," Shirley chuckled. "Anyway, I believe he intended it to be a home for local artifacts, exhibits, and things like that."

"It might not be such a bad idea to make room for a museum." Billie surveyed the room thoughtfully, her mind already drumming up ideas. "Having it in the basement might not be such a good idea, however."

"Why not?"

"Normally the dampness and mold would work against it. However, my impression is that this building seems to have good air circulation and temperature control, judging by the condition of the items already here. Look at that rope."

She turned back to the item and held it up for Shirley's inspection. "Your husband said it's made of natural fibers, and yet it shows only minor fraying and deterioration. Plus, there are some benefits to a basement setting, such as no direct exposure to sunlight, which can be fatal to old photographs. So, maybe it's worth considering. Meanwhile, we could create a temporary display of what we already have, something that would highlight the library's link to the mill." Billie dropped the rope and brushed off her hands. "That raises another question. Do we have any room for a display?"

"Let me think." Shirley ran her fingers across her chin. "What about out front, on that big porch of ours? It would be close to their natural environment, so to speak."

"Let's do it. Meanwhile, I'll put on my agenda the idea of a permanent museum. Now, for these boxes of books, I—"

"Billie, it's time to go home." Shirley drew out her words, as if reminding an excited child, a grin lighting her face.

Billie laughed, yet couldn't resist reaching for a box. "There could be a big surprise in one of these. How about if I just take a peek in this one?"

"That would be like me eating one potato chip."

"I guess you're right," she sighed, forcing her hands back to her side. "Let's go."

"And Billie," Shirley added, catching her attention while turning to leave. "I think the library is in good hands."

"I hope so, Shirley. I hope so."

Beneath her breath, Billie muttered a fervent wish that she prove herself worthy of Shirley's faith.

Chapter Three

Altogether, it wasn't a bad first week, though based on what standard, Billie could not say. As far as she could determine, there were no budding revolts among the volunteers or public, no formal or informal communications from the mayor pointing out the errors of her ways, and if there were, no local media around to pounce upon them.

Much of her time she spent in the library's public service areas, listening and learning from the staff and patrons alike. Early on she'd decided there would be no major decisions before she had the chance to gather some feedback, something slow in coming. At the most, thirty to fifty people would enter the library a day, including those who were there to attend scheduled events in the meeting room.

She found a bright spot in the small group of children who came for a weekly story hour conducted by a volunteer named Loretta Collins, a woman in her sixties, who appeared far too elegant in dress and demeanor for a rural setting like Woodland Hills. Nonetheless, the kids loved her reverse Pinocchio impersonation, a woman who turned into a puppet. It obviously was a carryover from her days as a puppet-show producer. From beginning of a story to end, she would jab her arms and contort her head in sharply angled movements, much to the delight of the youngsters.

Yes, Billie had survived the first week, even took advantage of the tranquil pace to set up, with Shirley's help, the old mill exhibit on the porch. An appropriate touch, she'd concluded. The community had grown up around the mill, which not only spawned it, but sustained it through its early development. Now the library had become part of the legacy, an institution viewed in much the same manner as the friendly neighbor next door.

At week's end she prepared to turn her attention from the people to the land, the enduring influence in the lives of southern Missouri residents, as she had come to learn from random conversation. She wanted to get a feel for the place fast wrapping itself around her heart.

"To get a real feel for this land, you need to get on a horse," her uncle advised.

She hadn't been topside of one since her childhood and then it was only on one of those ponies that, for a dollar, circled a ring like an automaton.

"Here, take a look at this." He handed her a small chapbook that served as the community's phone book. "I think there's a ridin' stable east of town, if I'm not mistaken."

She flipped through nearly all of the yellow pages before lighting her finger on "Stables," under the listing. "Countryside Stables–boarding–instruction–trail rides."

"Is that the one?" she asked, a curious combination of excitement and dread rippling through her at the thought of learning to ride.

"I think so. It's about twenty-five miles down the road from here. You know where the Buzzard's Roost Saloon is?"

"I've seen it."

"It's about two miles past it. There's a sign that will point you in the right direction." Her uncle looked at her quizzically. "Goin' alone?"

"Do you want to get on a horse?" she asked earnestly. Having a companion would make the adventure more pleasant.

"Nope, so I guess you're goin' alone." He winked at her, his eyes crinkled with amusement. "You might want to give them a call, see what time their next trail ride is."

"I believe I will take a look at the place first, to see if it offers something more than a trot around a paddock."

And to gauge whether she could really get up the nerve for something she'd never done that didn't involve books.

Early Saturday she was a mile out of Woodland Hills and settled into the rhythm of the road, banking off one curve and into the next, bobbing from hill to hollow. In the distance, wisps of fog rose from the blue-green valleys below to hilltop height elevated by the warmth of the sun's morning rays. She cracked the windows of her truck to drink in the purified air, her spirits soaring with the glory of the day.

The neon buzzard mounted high above the saloon, though unlit, came into view a mile away, giving her adequate time to scan the passing roadside for the signpost. Unfortunately, it turned out to be nothing more than a warped wood shingle attached to the stump of a dead tree, causing her to almost overshoot it. She abruptly hit the brakes and skidded into a left turn, leaving her truck planted at the bottom of a dry creek bed running alongside the access road.

Billie paused to regain her bearings. Glancing again at the sign, she fishtailed out of the creek bed and began a rollicking ride down a stretch of dirt road paralleling a rock ridge. A few yards ahead she saw another makeshift sign with an arrow pointing in the direction of a gravel road.

She made the turn, and worked her way up a steep incline to a level portion from where she could see a rust red barn sitting on a rise a short distance up the road. Across the creek bottom from the barn sat a modest white-frame house.

Billie pulled her truck off the road onto a dirt siding, switched off the engine, and sat for a moment, listening to the light gusts of wind whisk down the hillsides, and waving clouds of dust out of her face.

No one was in sight, so she decided to take a closer look. She hopped from her truck and, as if on signal, a loud yapping commenced.

A small dog of mixed breed stood positioned halfway between her and the barn, doing its best to look ferocious. As she approached the entrance, the pet increased the intensity of its bark, back-peddling with each fresh outburst.

"Tripwire–knock it off!" came a command from a deep male voice inside the barn.

The dog stopped its barking and she halted her approach, both of them switching their attention from each other to the barn's entrance, from where a slender man strolled out of the shadow and into the sunlight. He was considerably taller and somewhat older than she and dressed in traditional country garb, from the red flannel shirt, straw cowboy hat, and worn blue jeans to the well-trodden boots.

"Hello. Cory Winslow," he said by way of introduction, extending his hand.

"Billie Staley." She accepted his hand.

A firm hand, attached to an even firmer body, with a face cured, cleaned, and tanned to go with it.

"I hope Tripwire wasn't much of a bother." He lifted his hat to run his hands through curly, light brown hair.

She chuckled. "Appropriate name."

"Yeah, he can belt out an alarm alright. He just doesn't know when to shut it off. He even gets on the other dogs' nerves."

"You have others?" She looked warily around the yard,

expecting to be pounced on at any moment.

"A couple of old hounds to chase off the coons, and also a couple of cats to take care of the rodents." He wiped his sweaty brow with a handkerchief, before stuffing it in his back pocket. "So what brings you up this way?"

"Well, I'm new to the area and according to my uncle, the best way to learn the lay of the land is on horseback." She stuffed her hands in her pocket, feeling a bit awkward and out of her element. "So, I found your name in the phone book and decided to come take a look."

His hazel eyes wrinkled at the corners with his smile. "I'm glad to hear somebody checks that phonebook. You must live in Woodland Hills."

"Yes, I do."

"And you want to take a trail ride."

"Well, yes," she paused, clearing her throat, "I was thinking about doing that at some point."

"How about right now?"

"Now?" she exclaimed, a mixture of excitement and nervousness creeping into her voice.

"Sure. I was about ready to go out on my own when you pulled up. Our next scheduled ride is not until tomorrow afternoon. So, you're welcome to come along with me."

"How much is your fee?"

"Thirty bucks an hour but since you're not getting the official thing, I'll cut that in half." He turned back to the barn, rummaging through some gear near the door.

"Where does the trail lead?" she asked, her attention drawn to an elderly woman who'd exited the adjacent house to shake the dust from a throw rug.

"It leads that way." He nodded in the direction of the house.

"Do you live there?"

"With my grandparents, yes," he answered, a wry smile revealing his awareness of the debate being waged in her head.

"Okay," she said, "but I have to warn you, it's been years since I've been on a horse."

"That's what I'm here for."

He faced her again, arms folded across his chest, as though awaiting her next reaction.

"Is it safe to leave my purse in the truck?"

"Probably so, but if it makes you feel better, you might want to lock it."

"I think I'll do that," she said, back-stepping toward her truck.

"While you're doing that, I'll throw a saddle on another mount," he called after her.

Billie stuck her purse under the front seat, taking a moment to check her face in the review mirror. As was often the case since her parents' death, she could not help but note their reflection in her blend of red hair, freckles, and green eyes.

She shut the windows and locked the doors, at the same time weighing what a fool she might turn out to be. Granted, he looked nice, but to trek off into the woods with a complete stranger went against her better judgment. She glanced at the house on her way back up the hill, wondering in jest if his grandparents might be willing to go along for the ride. Still, a man who lived with his grandparents couldn't be all bad.

He stepped from the barn with reins in each hand. Trailing behind him were a prancing black stallion, and to her astonishment, a plodding mule.

"You look surprised," he said, with a twinkle of amusement in his eyes.

"That is a mule, is it not?"

"You're learning fast. She's a boarder. Belongs to a Canadian who spends his summers up north. You needn't worry, though. Florence—the mule—is for me. Houdini here is for you." He handed her the reins.

"Why Houdini?"

"Why the name or why for you?"

"Why the name."

"He keeps trying to escape the barn by nibbling at the locks. Not to burst any romantic ideas some people might have, but the fact is, a horse can be destructive. They can chew up or trample anything within their reach."

"He seems pleasant enough to me." She affectionately stroked the animal's forehead.

"Houdini has a good temperament, despite his occasional mischief-making." He glanced at her out of the corner of his eye as he adjusted the horse's straps. "Who he's around has a lot to do with his behavior. He needs to feel comfortable like he does with you."

"How do you know that?" she asked, continuing her caressing.

"If he wasn't he'd be back-stepping with his ears pinned back or shuffling his hooves. Notice the rhythmic way he's swishing his tail? If he was unhappy, he'd be swinging it every which way. Here, give him one of these and he will be even happier." He handed her a mint from his pocket.

She raised her hand level to the horse's mouth and felt the tickle of a tongue on her palm, as the animal nibbled at the offering.

"Whoops!" she yelped, as the horse bobbed his face into hers.

"And when he begins to smooch, that's really a good

sign," he added with a wink.

"That mule of yours doesn't seem all that excited."

"She's not." He shrugged. "This is a regular regimen for her. She's out to do her exercise, not out to have fun. You ready?"

"I suppose. Like I said, it's been a while. Do I—"

"Step to the left side of the horse and grab the saddle horn with your left hand. You can grab another part of the saddle with your right, if you wish. That's it. Now put your left foot in the stirrup."

She feigned a disgusted look at the notion she needed to be told which foot to mount the horse with.

"Now swing yourself up."

She did and immediately felt the stirring of powerful bones and muscle beneath her, as the animal adjusted to its rider with a series of sidesteps. She instinctively reached to pat the horse's mane, until he returned to a near standstill. Settled, she swiveled to see Cory mounted on Florence a few yards behind her.

The guy doesn't belong on a mule. Sancho Panza, yes, but not him.

"Ready?" he asked.

"Ready as I'll ever be."

"Remember, to go right you give a little tug on the reins to the right. The same for a left turn. To stop him, just pull back on the reins." He demonstrated the moves, much like a flight attendant giving pre-flight safety instructions. "Houdini doesn't need much direction, only little reminders about when to stop and go. He's very familiar with these trails."

"So, which way are we headed?" She covered her eyes with one hand, looking off into the distance, her insides churning with expectation.

"Just follow that footpath ahead of you. Okay? Now give him a tap with your heels."

She did as instructed and the stallion broke into a slow walk.

They traveled the footpath in a semi-circular route across the creek bed and around the house to where it joined with a larger dirt path.

"Is this a road?" she called back to him.

"Once was."

"Where does it lead?"

"Nowhere. It ends about a half-mile down. We think it may have been the beginning of a lumber route years back. For some reason, it wasn't completed, maybe because the company lost their logging rights in the middle of its construction. Some say it was because of a shady deal that went bust. That's why it got the name Shady Lane."

"Not because of the trees?"

"Nope."

She gazed overhead at the backward march of overhanging limbs and the dance of sunlight on fluttering tips of leaves.

"What kind of trees are these?" she asked, as he advanced alongside her.

"Mostly short leaf pine with some oak and elm mixed in. Right now they are not in the best of shape. They could use some moisture."

"How long has it been since it last rained? I know there has been none in the time I've been here."

"Except for a few sprinkles, it' been unusually warm and dry. Funny part is, the northern part of the state is getting quite a bit. It just hasn't reached down here."

"Is this road normally this crusty?" she asked, above the

clack of hooves.

"Yeah. Actually, the whole terrain in these parts isn't very fertile–plenty of rock and only a thin layer of topsoil. That's why you don't see much farming around here. When the sawmills all started going out of business back in the thirties, a lot of people, like my grandparents, hung around to try and make some kind of living off the land."

His gaze followed the course of a far-off buzzard. "Not too many could make a go of it. Consequently, most of the young people took off elsewhere, which thinned out the population fast. If there is any farming, it's usually not crops but animals–dairy cattle, chickens, hogs–even a couple of ostrich farms."

"What about the wild kind?" She gazed off into the woods, as if some species might suddenly appear on cue.

"Plenty of deer, wild turkey, some wild hogs, a few black bears, and an assortment of others, from buzzards to bats."

"Bats?"

"Yes. You have bats in the city, right? Aren't you a city gal?"

"Whatever would make you think that," she said slyly, glancing sideways at him.

"My business attracts mostly city folk."

"Is that a bad thing?"

"Not today."

The compliment caught her by surprise, quieting her for the moment.

They reached the end of the road. She easily could imagine a foreman in a time past standing at the exact same spot, announcing to a weary work crew that they drop what they were doing, that the road project was being called off.

"Now where?" she asked her suddenly silent companion.

"To your left there is a narrow trail leading to the bottom of the hill and the river."

"How far down is it?"

"About six hundred feet." He watched for her reaction, a hint of a challenge lurking within his gaze.

"Isn't it kind of steep?" she asked, standing in her stirrups for a glimpse down the incline. Unfortunately, she'd never been one to refuse a challenge.

"Nothing Houdini or you can't handle."

"You seem to have more confidence in me than I have." The swirl of excitement and nervousness again welled within her.

He laughed, a soothing low chuckle. "Your natural reaction as you head down will be to lean back in the saddle and stiffen your legs in the stirrups. That's fine. Let the horse travel at its own pace. You don't need to be yanking at the reins. Remember, you're just along for the ride."

Billie tapped the animal's flanks, nudging it forward. Carefully, the horse began its step-by-step descent, first pawing with a hoof before dropping his full weight. With every stride, bits of wood or rock would crackle, dislodge, and scatter. Now and then she felt the horse briefly lose its footing before quickly regaining it. Each time she would glance to her rear, only to see Cory with a hint of a smile on his face.

"Do you see it down there?" he called at one point.

"See what?" she asked apprehensively.

"The Jacks Fork."

"Oh, great."

"You don't seem excited."

"Right now, my eyes are glued to the trail immediately in front of me, so how can I get excited over something at the bottom of the hill?" she bellowed back.

She did, however, see her first wild animals, as two squirrels scurried from her path and into the brush.

Finally, the slope leveled off and she glimpsed the river through a last ridge of trees.

"Eureka!" she yelled, loud enough to twitch Houdini's ears.

From where they exited the woods, they were no more than ten yards from the water's edge. Any lingering anxieties she may have had from the trek down were quickly dissipated by the vista afforded her.

As far downstream as she could see, dense groves of trees hugged the river's banks, and rising above them, like nature's redoubts, sheer rock walls, their crevices embossed with mosses and ferns.

Cory drew up silently beside her. "Worth the ride down?"

"I'd say so." She forced her gaze from the majestic scenery to her obviously knowledgeable guide. "How did the Jacks Fork get its name?"

"According to old timers, it was named for a Shawnee Indian named Captain Jack who used to camp along the river with his tribes."

"It's sure not the traditional Indian name I associate with rivers."

"Let's cross." He tightened his reigns and clicked to his mule. "There's a nice shady spot on the far side where we can take a break."

"How deep is the water?"

"No more than knee deep. The larger the gravel bars, the less the water is a pretty good rule of thumb," he said, guiding Florence into the river.

She followed him across the narrow channel to a knoll shaded in part by a lone elm, rising majestically from the brown embankment.

"Have a seat," he said, taking the reins of the two animals and looping them around the nearest limb.

Doubtless he meant a seat on the dead tree trunk that, from the looks of the number of initials carved on it, served as a popular resting post for onlookers.

"So, Billie, how did you end up in Woodland Hills?" He took a seat beside her.

"A job. I'm the new director of the public library."

"They got a library there?"

"Yes. As a matter of fact, it's right on the river. I would guess about twenty to twenty-five miles downstream from where we sit." She pointed off in the distance.

"Is that right? I've been up and down this river too many times to count and I don't recall seeing a library."

"The building we are in was once a mill."

"The rust-colored building?"

"That's it."

"Yeah, so it's now a library. You must read a lot."

"Quite a bit. How about you?"

"Maybe I shouldn't admit this, but I haven't cracked a book since high school. I'll glance at a magazine every now and then, but someone would sure be right in saying I don't have a lot of book sense. Horse sense, yes—book sense, no."

Billie turned to better examine her companion, it suddenly occurring to her that he couldn't be more different from her. "What has horse sense taught you?"

"What's it taught me? It's taught me the land needs seasons, the animals need feed, and people need figuring out."

"And why do they need figuring out?" she asked, admittedly surprised and intrigued by his insight.

"Probably because I'm not around them a whole lot, not

like with horses. When a guy spends seven days a week cleaning them, grooming them, and feeding them, not to mention tending to their medical needs, he doesn't have much time left to deal with people."

"When you're required to deal with them, like on your trail rides, what are you looking for?"

"How they relate to the land and the animals."

"Those seem to be sensitive subjects in this area," she said, believing she was about to tap some inner feelings.

"You got it. Land and animals are the politics and religion of this entire region. A fellow may not know much about caring for them, but he best treat them with respect when he's around them." He turned his gaze from their grazing mounts to look at her directly. "That's pretty much how I try and figure people out–how they relate to the land and animals."

"How long have you been doing this?"

"Since I left high school. I took the business over from my grandparents. If you're wondering about my parents, they gave me up as a baby for reasons I'm not sure of, and I don't really care to know."

"Are they still in your life?"

"Not in my life nor in my grandparents' lives." He glanced back at the animals. "Last I heard they were living down in Florida somewhere, but not together. Apparently, they split and took off in separate directions with new partners."

"Are you married?"

"Nope. All the pretty girls hightail it out of here, as soon as they can. In fact, they don't even have to be pretty to hightail it."

"You must meet women on your trail rides."

"Yes ma'am, all kinds. College coeds, widowed, divorced. Most of 'em have that romantic girls-and-horse thing going when they arrive. You can see it in their eyes. They're ready to hop on a horse and ride off into the sunset, never to return. But, after an hour or so, their butt starts hurting, the romance begins to fade, and they're ready to return to their old ways."

He shrugged, as though it was standard behavior. "How about you—you married?"

"No."

"What city did you say you were from?"

"I didn't say, but it's St. Louis."

He pushed his hat back on his head. "Something wrong with the guys in St. Louis?"

"No. I think it has more to do with me and what you were saying about an hour of romance." She sighed. "I was in business there with my parents, the kind that required frequent travel. My socializing consisted mainly of an occasional wine and cheese party where I might meet a man, exchange business cards, and then head off in a different direction. That's not good for someone who doesn't believe in long-distance relationships."

"Sounds like you wanted to settle down in one place."

"Not necessarily. I always felt moving to a new town would be an adventuresome thing."

"In what way?"

"Making new friends, meeting new challenges."

"Is that why you left the business?"

To another person, at another time, she might have been reluctant to answer the question. "No, my parents were killed in a plane crash, and rather than continue the business, which would have been a load to carry without them, I decided to change careers. So, here I am, a world away, sitting with you in the middle of these hills."

"Really sorry about your parents—but not sorry about you

sitting here." He covered her hand with his, drawing her attention. "Do you know how to swim?"

"Swim?" she repeated, setting off a tiny alarm bell in her head before answering. "Yes, I can swim."

"It's not what you're thinking," he quickly added, before a loud bray from Florence interrupted their conversation. "She's telling us it's time to go."

He dropped her hand and rose. "I'm afraid she's getting to know the routine too well."

Billie couldn't help but wonder what routine Florence knew too well. And what had led her to reveal so much? She was usually not that free with people on first meeting them.

They followed the river deeper downstream, through an array of trees and rock formations.

"See that cave across the way?" he called from ahead, his voice halfway to an echo.

"Yes," she called back, spotting its opening close by the bank.

"That's a bat cave."

"Yuk!"

"Don't worry. They're not vampire bats out to suck your blood. These only eat insects."

"What's that across its opening?"

"A gate."

"For what?" She shielded her eyes to examine the gate better. "With that spacing, it's not going to keep the bats in or out."

He chuckled. "It's to keep the people out."

"Who would want to go in there?"

"Kids. They were holding their rituals and initiations there at night, upsetting both the bats and the parents, so the state put up a gate."

"You, I'm sure, were never one of those kids."

"Yes ma'am, I sure was." He winked at her over his shoulder. "You should hear the whoosh of those invisible wings as they zoom by your ears."

She shuddered. "That's one call of nature I can do without."

"You won't see or hear them this time of the day. In the evening you can hear them begin to chirp. That's the first sign that they're beginning to stir. Later on a few of the bats—scouts—will fly out of the cave to see what's cookin'. It isn't long after whole batches of them come flying out."

"So, they're not blind after all."

"Nope."

"Good for them, but good for us? I'm not so sure."

A short stretch of bank later, they came upon a nook formed by a semi-circle of boulders, washed smooth by decades of overflows. She watched as Cory dismounted and walked with Florence in hand to the water's edge.

He was a man as comfortable in his element as he was in his snug jeans.

"Here's where we cross to pick up a second trail that will take us back up the slope to Shady Lane. The water is a little deeper here, but it's only about twenty-five yards across and very still compared to what it can be at times."

"How deep?" she asked from atop Houdini, a note of anxiety creeping back into her voice.

"About seven or eight feet."

"You think I can handle that?"

"The horse can," he deadpanned, before arching one teasing brow. "Besides, why should it matter if you take a little dip into the drink, now that we both know you can swim?"

For a moment, she pondered the challenge, her thoughts

interrupted by the sight of a large bird executing lazy eights above an overhead cliff.

"What's that?" She pointed skyward.

"A turkey buzzard."

"Well that's a good sign–buzzards and bats. Whatever happened to the deer and the antelope?"

He grinned. "Probably hiding. Ready?"

"Okay, but I'm taking off my shoes first."

"The horse isn't taking his off," he said casually, mounting his mule.

Billie reached down and slipped off her sneakers and socks, fastened the laces together, and wrapped them around the saddle horn. She then furled her jeans above the knee line, exposing legs she knew had not seen sunlight since God knows when.

"Ready?" he asked again, as an impatient husband or beau might ask of a woman primping for a night out.

"Ready." She took a deep breath, fortifying her nerves.

"Don't rush him and steer his head straight with the reins. When you reach the far bank, you're going to go uphill quickly, so put the reins in one hand and with your other, grab a handful of his mane. I'll be right behind you," he said, motioning her to cross.

Houdini needed but a tap before stepping gingerly down the embankment and into the water, pausing for a quick drink. As he continued ahead, she could feel the first tingle of water on her toes.

"Water's cool," she called out, keeping her eyes glued ahead.

"Many of the rivers in this part of the country are spring-fed. They run cooler than normal."

She was close to five yards out when the stallion sprung

the full weight of its body forward into the stream, sending a rush of water up her legs and across her waistline. But for the horse's head and her upper torso, they were completely immersed, the weight of the horse beneath her replaced by a buoyancy that lifted her body to an exhilarated state and her mind off the fact that she needn't have shed her shoes or rolled up her pants.

As the stallion heaved ahead, she instinctively urged it forward with pelvic thrusts, until it regained its footing a minute later on the streambed below. They were only a few feet from dry ground, when she clutched both reins in her left hand and latched on to Houdini's moistened mane with the right for the final lurch up the embankment.

Back on solid ground, she patted Houdini on the neck, as he shook remnants of water from his coat. The river lay behind them but the adrenaline continued to flow. She felt more alive than she could remember since her parents' deaths.

"How'd I do?" she shouted out, pivoting in the saddle to catch a glimpse of Cory and Florence behind her. What she saw instead was Cory standing chest-high in the middle of the stream with a bemused grin on his face.

"What's going on? What happened? Where's Florence?" she feverishly asked.

The answer came a moment later, as the tips of two large ears broke through the water's surface, followed by the remainder of the mule's head.

He sat there on Florence, as though nothing out of the ordinary had happened. "She decided to walk it today."

"I can't believe—"

"It can happen," he said, emerging from the stream. "She has a mind of her own."

"If only I had a camera."

"Then she might not have done it." He guided the mule toward the foot of the hillside and the opening of the trail.

"This will take us back up to Shady Lane," he said, taking the lead. "This time you lean forward in the saddle instead of back, okay?"

She gave her horse all the slack he needed on the route up, managing to stay in sync with his strides, grabbing the saddle horn to steady herself whenever he temporarily lost footing.

As best she could tell, they re-entered Shady Lane near its halfway point where Cory maneuvered his mule a neck in front of Houdini.

"Prepare yourself," he called back over his shoulder. "Houdini is now going to take his instructions from Florence."

"How's that?"

"These are herd animals. They follow the leader." He nudged his mount.

The mule broke into a trot and as if by reflex Houdini followed. The jarring up-and-down motion caused her to lose her center of gravity. To correct the imbalance, she stood in the stirrups long enough to realign her feet. The moment she started to adjust to the gait, Cory launched them into a cantor.

Instantly, the rhythmic forward-and-back motion relieved her concern, not to mention her butt. Once more, she found herself floating on a new sensation, a convergence of mind and emotion, muscle and bone. She knew, at any moment, another jab of Cory's heels would send them into a full gallop and her spirits even higher.

The best was not to be, however, as ahead of them, framed by the end of the lane, appeared the house on the hill where they eased their mounts to a walk and onto the path back to the barn.

"Sorry about the wet clothes," he said upon arrival.

"A small price to pay." She pulled self-consciously on her wet shirt where it clung to her chest. "Which reminds me, I owe you some money."

She handed him the reins, unhooked her shoes from the saddle horn, started to put them on, but then decided to jog to her truck bare-footed to retrieve her purse.

She paid him and thanked him and was about to leave when she heard him say matter-of-factly, "Houdini wants to know if you're coming back next week."

"Oh, he does?" she replied, stroking the animal's forehead, feeling heat rising in her cheeks.

"He thinks you are a natural."

"What does that mean?"

"Few lessons required."

She risked a glance in his direction, only to catch him with a lazy grin on his face. "You're not one of those horse whisperers, are you?"

"He's the one who does the whispering."

She puckered her lips in thought. "What time is your Sunday trail ride?"

"He's talking about the Saturday morning workout with me. He says to look at it as a date, with him picking up the tab."

"Oh, okay," she said, at once pleased and surprised.

"Nice meeting you, Billie." He kept his eyes fixed on her, as if awaiting her next reaction.

"And you, Cory." She backtracked a few feet, before bounding off to her truck and home.

She related her memories of the morning to her uncle over dinner, who occasionally punctuated her narrative with the comment, "wasn't that a bit risky?" Later, she took them to bed with her, welcoming other images to fill her mind and charge her imagination—until a shrill whistle scattered them like children from a playground.

Again, the murmur of male voices, this time closer at hand, prodded her from bed and to the window...to a vision of blackened space.

What were they doing back there? The same impulse which led her to seek out a rare book in the farthest corner of a used bookstore, now propelled her to find out what business the militia had so near her uncle's property.

She shed her nightshirt and slipped into jeans, sweatshirt, and sneakers, and then into the cool night. Buster greeted her, but she confined the animal to the cabin, fearing its blithe manner not in keeping with her stealth intentions, foolhardy though they may be.

Still, once outside, the murmurs seemed distant enough that she felt like she could risk a closer look without endangering herself.

She entered the edge of the woods toward the direction of the voices. Aided by a full moon, her eyes swiftly adjusted to the dark. She could make out the trees and bushes nearest her, but anything beyond appeared as shadows, except for the space directly above her where the moon and stars ignited the night sky.

With each step the leaves crunched beneath her feet, though fortunately the evening dew already had settled them, muffling the noise. How heightened was the scent of the forest come nightfall, she thought, as odors of moss and decomposing leaves satiated the atmosphere.

She searched the landscape for shapes to match the sounds, when, faraway, she discerned broken beams of light, darting back and forth, moving in unison to a chorus of commands. Flashlights–men marching double-time, as the clamor faded further into the trees.

Quiet returned to the forest, followed by the familiar symphony of crickets, cicadas, and frogs, which brought, in turn, a sensibility to her mind. Any advance further and she easily could become lost, left to the mercy of man and beast alike.

She returned home to the spontaneous smooches of a welcoming pet, to her own space, to the comfort of her bed, and to the pleasant dreams of the day past.

Chapter Four

There had been an upturn in the number of individuals volunteering their time to assist in the library's operation, and Billie wanted to think of it as an indicator of her acceptance by the community. The realist in her, however, suggested that the motives of the volunteers more likely had to do with either an eagerness to relieve domestic boredom, a craving to share talents, or a basic need to socialize.

Mainly, they were older residents, except for Scott McKinley, an earnest-eyed, floppy-haired, floppier-dressed youngster who, when not lending the staff a helping hand, spent half his day as a high school student and the other half as a library lizard. His offers to assist with nearly any project seldom passed without a taker. In addition to an unquenchable curiosity, he possessed a variety of natural gifts, not the least of which was a strong back, a necessity for her basement project.

"You see these boxes?" she asked, sweeping her hand in their direction. "They're filled with books. I'd like for you to help me go through them. That means unpacking and sorting."

"Into what?" he asked, wiping an unruly lock of hair from his eyes.

"Two piles," she answered. "One for those we'll put into a book sale and one for those we'll consider adding to the collection."

"Shirley mentioned there might be some rare books mixed in," he said, a hopeful note in his voice.

"If there are–and that's a very big if–then we'll put them in a third pile," she said with a coy smile, not wanting to dampen his enthusiasm.

"How many books do you suppose there are?" His interested gaze swept the room.

"Oh, it looks as if there may be two hundred boxes. Figuring an average of about 25 books per box, that would put the total at nearly five thousand volumes."

"Do you want me to unpack them all first?"

He seemed undaunted. Youth.

"Why don't we do them a box at a time. That way we can re-box them immediately and save some space. Many will require only a glance, meaning we'll not have to take them out of the box at all."

Scott removed the first box from the top of the pile and placed it in an open workspace between the two chairs they would work from.

"How can you tell if a book is rare, Miss Staley?" he asked, as they began the sorting routine.

"First rule to remember is that old doesn't necessarily mean rare." She pulled a box closer, examining the spines facing up. "A more accurate barometer–or maybe I should say a better starting barometer–is the old law of supply and demand, and even then the demand must exceed the supply. A book can meet all the other criteria of a rare book, but if no one wants it, then it doesn't qualify. To complicate matters further, demand alone does not make a book rare."

"Then what exactly does?" He ripped open the top of a box.

"Its significance more than anything–whether it represents an important edition of a major historical or literary work. There are other factors also, such as special binding, unique illustrations, whether it is an autographed copy." She glanced at the first group of titles he passed to her.

"Where do you find most of them?"

"Attics, auctions, basements, catalogs, garages, you name it. What you have to keep in mind is that these kinds of places are not conducive to maintaining a well-conditioned book, which definitely counts in determining its value. That's why many rare books are discovered in private collections."

The first two boxes she marked "book sale," while only one of the books from the initial batch went into the "library collection" category.

"That's going into the collection?" He looked up from his books sorting, his eyes alight with interest.

"Possible addition," she replied. "It's probably a duplicate of a title we already have, but it may be in better condition. If so, we'll do a swap."

The original pile of boxes slowly shrunk, as they busily worked their way through them. Many contained sets of encyclopedias, usually with a volume or two missing. Others were stuffed with Readers Digest condensed books or collections of National Geographic magazines.

"Here you go," he said, holding up to her a copy of *Don Quixote*.

Her eyes drifted from the artist's cover rendering of the mock hero, resplendent in his cast of armor, to the image of his faithful servant, Sancho Panza, atop his donkey, looking nothing like her Saturday morning squire.

"You're thinking that's a first edition?" She arched an eyebrow.

"No, just a favorite of mine, but it is in good condition, right?" He passed it carefully to her, the hope evident in his eyes.

"Yes, it very much is," she replied. "What is sad is

finding that intrinsically important book, one you're saying to yourself, "*I've found it,*" only to discover it has some loose or missing pages, is torn somewhere, has a personal library marking on it, or it has been rebound–the list goes on."

Before he could pop her another question, she decided to sneak in one of her own. "What do you think of the library, Scott?"

"This library?" He shrugged. "Oh, it's fine."

"Do you have a computer at home?"

"My folks and I share one."

"What do you think of computers in a library?" She watched him intently for his reaction.

"Yeah, I heard about that from one of the volunteers–no computers in the library. That was what the previous owner wanted, wasn't it?" He stretched to retrieve another box.

Obviously it wasn't as important an issue for him as for Mr. Whitington or Chad Jenkins.

"What the previous librarian wanted."

"Right, sorry." He flushed slightly. "I don't know. I guess I haven't thought that much about it."

"What are you hearing from the other residents? Is it much of an issue?"

"To be honest, no. They pretty much go with the flow. Why? You thinking of putting them in?"

She paused. The matter required more thought, and the input of others. "Let's say it's under consideration."

"I guess it really doesn't matter to me one way or the other. I have the computer at home and we have them at school, so it's not like there are none available. I come to this library for the books, because I like browsing through them. Others may have a different opinion. I heard one of my instructors at school say books would become less useful for looking up information as computers take over. Do you think that?"

No books someday? The thought sent a shiver through her. "I think there will always be a place in our lives for books."

"So, when do you have to decide?"

"Soon."

He looked up from the box in front of him, focusing his gaze on her. "The way I look at it, Miss Staley, is that you were the one appointed to run the library, so it's your decision."

She closed the book she'd been thumbing through. "What if the decision is opposite the public's opinion? Remember, this is their library."

He nodded thoughtfully. "Right, that's a good point, but isn't it the same issue facing elected officials? Are they elected to carry out our wishes, or are they elected to do what they think is best?"

Clearly, he was a youth who already knew how to think for himself. He reminded her of herself at his age. "Vote their conscience, you're saying."

"That's the way my civics teacher puts it, though he feels they prefer to do an end run by muddling things up."

She sighed. "If only the line in the sand was not so clearly drawn, I—"

"Billie, are you down there?" came the call from Shirley, leaning her head through the open basement doorway.

"Yes."

"There are some people here who want to talk to you."

"Okay, I'm on my way," she yelled back, tossing the books she had in hand into the burgeoning book sale pile.

She instructed Scott to continue, believing he already had exhibited a knack for the routine and, if need be, could set aside the questionable titles for her decision.

"Where are they?" she asked Shirley on her arrival at the circulation desk.

"They're in the parking lot. They said they would wait for you there."

"Who are they?" she asked, puzzled at the development.

"Billie, I may be wrong, but I think they are members of that local militia group," Shirley replied reluctantly. "I think they want to use our meeting room." She shook her head.

"Oh, that's great."

"I gave them a copy of our meeting room policy. They took it outside to read. Do you want me to tell them you're here?"

"No, I'll do that," she said, running the options through her head, knowing the importance of meeting potential problems head on, before they mushroomed into big ones.

Garbed in camouflage fatigues and boots, they easily could have been mistaken for soldiers from nearby Fort Leonard Wood on leave from recent maneuvers. Their manner and features revealed otherwise, however. One leaned on the fender of her truck, gangly arms and legs crossed, his sleepy eyes awakening to her arrival, his smirk indicating his anticipation.

His two companions, one short, beady-eyed, and shorn to the scalp, and the other of medium height, square shoulders, protruding chin, and receding hair, stood side by side a few yards away. The beady-eyed one was looking over the shoulder of his cohort, who was busily scanning what appeared to be the meeting room policy.

"I understand you wanted to see me," she said as a way of introduction to the two. "And sir, do you mind? That's my truck you're sitting on," she called to the third, who shot a glance at the policyholder before abandoning his leaning post.

"Yes ma'am, we're interested in your meeting room," the square-shouldered one and apparent leader said, adopting a more formal tone. "I see here it's available to local organizations."

"The name of your organization is?"

"The Southern Missouri Free Militia."

"And the purpose of your organization?"

"Like it says here," he said, pointing to the policy, "to educate and inform the citizens of the community." He held the paper out to her, as though she'd never seen it.

"Of what?" She ignored the gesture, keeping her eyes on him.

"Of us."

"How many will be in attendance?"

"Twenty to twenty-five–maybe more."

"Our meeting room holds a maximum of thirty."

"We'll keep it under that."

"As the policy states, there is no food, no collection of money to be taken, no disruption of regular library services, and no violation of any laws allowed."

"Agreed," he said, maintaining a proper manner in contrast to his companions, who appeared ready to burst into laughter.

"When did you need the meeting room?"

"Next Monday."

"Time?"

"Ten to noon should do it."

"I'll have to check the schedule to see if it's available," she said, hoping it was not the case.

"Your associate already checked. It's available. We also want to book it the first Monday of every month."

"It says in the policy that the room cannot be booked on a long-term basis. In other words, we don't permit regularly scheduled meetings." She had him on that one.

"I saw other groups marked in months in advance–didn't you fellows?" He asked, turning to the other two, who nodded in agreement.

"Those were either library-sponsored programs or programs co-sponsored by the library, which makes them exceptions."

"You could be our co-sponsor," he suggested, cracking a smile.

She crossed her arms in frustration. "I'm afraid it's not part of our mission."

"Let me get back to this one-time provision. It says here that the room cannot be booked more than a month ahead, which is what I take you mean by long term–that you can't book it say six months down the road."

"Correct."

"But we do have the option to reserve it on a month-by-month basis." A sly grin spread over his face. "In other words, after each of our meetings, we could book it for the following month, right?"

"Yes," she replied, realizing he had found a loophole, one she had failed to note in an earlier cursory reading. "But only if that same day and time is available and not already reserved."

"I don't think that is likely to happen, do you?"

"It's possible. By the way, I'm sure you also noticed that all meetings must be open to the general public."

"It's our meeting."

"And our rules."

"I'm sure the fellows would be happy for a lady like Miss

Staley to sit in on our meeting," the sleepy-eyed one called to his comrades.

"Pay no heed to him, ma'am. Sometimes, he gets carried away by the sight of a pretty woman, particularly if they show a little pluck. He likes to think he can tame them."

"Like he tamed that filly over in West Plains with some hard ridin'," the beady-eyed one chortled.

"I tell you, human flesh is so weak, especially his," the square-shouldered one said, shaking his head in feigned disgust.

Time to get this meeting to an end and the exchange back under her control. "You will need to fill out the attached application form and turn it in before the meeting. Okay?" she said tersely.

"Yes ma'am, we'll be sure and do that."

She turned and walked back to the library, the weight of their eyes upon her. Despite her misgivings, she felt she had no choice but to allow them use of the room. The library had no right to conducting background checks on organizations. Groups were presumed innocent until evidence of meeting-room misuse proved differently. As a precaution, she would notify the mayor of the situation.

"How is it going, Scott?" she asked upon rejoining him.

"Making some headway, I think. I've set aside a few for you." He tapped a small pile of books aside him.

They were mainly second-hand books, in good condition, but lacking that significant imprint, edition, or origin to set them apart, a judgment he took in stride.

"I'm running into a number of Bibles. What about them?" he asked.

"I'm sure you've heard no book has been published or read more than the Bible. That should tell you how few have any monetary value. The same holds true for most religious publications, since they usually were printed in mass quantities. The hope was they could be distributed to as many of the faithful as possible."

"And school books, what about those? There are quite a few I've come across."

"I don't mean to be discouraging, Scott, but as a general rule, a textbook would have to be at least a hundred years old to even give it a second look."

She leaned back from the pile she'd been sorting through, stretching her back. "Say, why don't we call it a day? We've made a sizable dent in that pile. How many would you say we have been through?"

"Close to 20 boxes," he replied, glancing about him. "I've got time to do a few more, if that's okay with you."

She chuckled. "I think that's enough for the day. As with many an endeavor, patience is mandatory in the used book trade. Plus we need to remember that our prime object here is not to find a rare book but clean out a basement, okay?"

"Okay," he said with a downcast eye.

She patted his shoulder and whispered, "It's okay. They'll all still be here waiting for you tomorrow."

Following work, Billie drove to the mayor's general store, hailing along the way the small-town perk of short commutes and angle parking. Posted on the store's sidewalk display window was an assemblage of colorful flyers announcing upcoming antique shows and craft fairs sponsored by surrounding community organizations.

Sidestepping an aging collie sunning itself near the entrance, she entered the establishment and immediately spotted Keating behind the checkout counter talking to a woman with bleached blond curls and multiple rings on fingers and ears.

He acknowledged her arrival with a conspicuous wave of the hand over the woman's shoulder. Rather than interrupt their chitchat, Billie decided to browse the store, a place that reminded her of the many stuffed-to-the-ceiling thrift stores she and her parents would rummage through in search of used books. Elongated tables, stacked with clothing and household goods, ran the entire length of the building's main room, bordered by adjacent alcoves bearing hunting and fishing equipment, foodstuffs, and other specialized products.

"Hey young lady!" the call came, accompanied by approaching footsteps of the mayor. "Stocking up on groceries?"

"No, my uncle insists on doing the grocery shopping," she replied, depositing the orange she had in hand back into one of the many bushels of fruit ringing the produce section.

"That Ray, he's a good ol' boy. Kind of quiet, though." He stopped just a few feet short of her, wearing a grin a size too big. "Say, how are things at the library? Have you reached a decision on the computer thing?"

"No, but there is a potential problem that came up today, which I thought should be brought to your attention."

"Oh, what's that? Somebody got too many overdue books?" he tittered.

"No, not that," she said deliberately, attempting to insert some decorum into the conversation. "We had a group today who made a request to reserve the library's meeting room."

"So?" he said, before she could continue.

"It was an organization called the Southern Missouri Free Militia."

"Oh, I see. The militia guys." He paused, his teasing

smile vanishing, as if she'd taken him slightly aback. "So, what did you tell them?"

She spread her hands in frustration. "I really had no choice, according to the meeting room policy. It clearly states that the room is available to community groups, as long as provisions of the policy are adhered to."

"Which say what?"

"Essentially, don't break any rules or laws and leave the room in the same condition you found it."

He rocked back on his heels. "So, the problem is what?"

"The problem is I am not familiar with the purpose of this particular outfit, but from what I have read, the activities of militia groups often border on the illegal. Are you aware if this is the case with these people?"

"Listen. Rumors about these militia people crop up on a regular basis, especially with the Waco thing going on. I've spotted a few of them in here on occasion. As far as I know, they haven't broken any laws."

"What concerns me the most is they intend to use the library on a regular basis." She cast a glance out the store window. "God forbid, if we should become a staging area for them."

"I tell you what." He pivoted around as he continued talking over his shoulder. "Let me give a call to Dan Booker over in Plainville–see what he thinks of the situation."

"Who is Dan Booker?" She followed him back to the checkout counter.

"The sheriff. Good guy for you to get to know." He picked up the phone and punched in a number he read off a card attached to a bulletin board.

"Yeah, this is Jake Keating over in Woodland Hills. Is the sheriff in? Sure, I'll hold."

He drummed his fingers on the counter and looked at Billie. "Nice outfit you have on there, Billie. I wish my wife could fit a dress like that—"

He must have caught her warning look as he quickly turned his attention back to the phone receiver. "Hey Dan, how ya doing? Good. Say, there's been a sticky situation develop here that I'd like to get your opinion on…Yeah, I know, it's the little ones that grow into the big ones. Well, my librarian here is telling me that the local militia guys have booked the library's meeting room and are planning on using it for their regular monthly meetings. Do you see any problems with that? Yeah, that's what I was saying. They've become a little stirred up lately, because of this Waco stuff going on…Right…Right…Right…Okay; I'll pass the word. Thanks Dan."

She waited for the word, hoping it would offer a magical way out of her predicament, if, in fact, he considered it one.

"Sheriff says just like you did, as long as they don't break any laws or any rules, there's not much that can be done." He patted her roughly on the shoulder. "He says it's your call. And that's what I say. Right now, I wouldn't read too much into it. As things stand, you're not their problem."

"Meaning they have no quarrel with me," she responded, recalling her uncle's words with the hope that the situation remain just that way.

She'd never banked on run-ins with local militia when she'd decided to move to the country. And she didn't want to start now.

Chapter Five

"Why the hell do you care? Chances are you'll be dead!"

"Mr. Stark, I don't believe that is what Mr. Hatch had in mind when he asked his question," Billie replied, her tone indicating her impatience. "I think he was asking for some assurance that his story, when it reaches its final form, will be his alone and will not be altered in any way, once he is no longer with us."

Ted Stark leaned back in his chair, his arms crossed mulishly across his chest. "Dead–that's what I said."

"Your oral history becomes part of your legacy, similar to a book. Some people–most people, I should say, do not wish for it to be tarnished or tampered with after it is completed."

"Which gets back to my question. Why would he care? He ain't going to be doing any worrying if he's dead."

"I don't think we want to take the discussion in that direction." Billie dug deep for some endurance. "Let me simply state there will be no altering of your tape, whether you're dead or alive."

"So, how are you going to stop that from happening?" Stark asked.

With relief, she reached for the papers in front of her. "Well, it just so happens that I did bring along some simple release forms for you to read and sign. Essentially, they state that you're granting your recorded memoir in its final form as a gift to the library for informational, educational, and scholarly purposes. In other words, you are placing it into the public record where it will remain as is. I apologize for not bringing this up at the first session and especially to you Mrs. Winfield, since we already have your story on tape."

"That's quite alright," she politely replied.

Billie passed out the release forms, which each signed and dated without further comment.

"Okay, Mr. Hatch, it's time for you to tell us your story," she said, drawing an audible sigh from Mr. Stark.

Jack Hatch straightened himself in his chair, hesitating a lengthy time before beginning, as though the import of what he was about to relate demanded clarity of thought.

"Okay. I grew up in Iowa where my two best buddies and I would spend most of our free time playing in the many fields located near our homes. We enjoyed the outdoors so much we eventually decided to join the Boy Scouts at the suggestion of our parents. By the end of high school, the three of us had made it to Eagle Scout."

"*Sheeet*! I could never make it past Tenderfoot—couldn't tie one of those damn square knots to save my life," Stark interjected. "Boy, were my parents pissed."

"Continue, Mr. Hatch," Billie said, second-guessing her decision to do the interviews as a group.

Casting a leery sideways glance at his group member, Hatch cleared his throat. "The three of us eventually decided we would enter Iowa State University together and major in forestry. One buddy wound up dropping out of school halfway through the program. The other buddy and I both made it through, though he decided to go into the lumber business following graduation. I chose instead to enter the U.S. Forest Service.

"I first was assigned as an intern at a ranger station in Washington State. Not long after, I applied for and got my first job as an Assistant Ranger in the Van Buren station."

"That's what–about thirty or forty miles from here?" she asked for her own edification.

He nodded. "That's right. Anyway, it's where I began my career as a ranger. However, it wasn't long before the problems began to—"

"Excuse me again for interrupting, Mr. Hatch, but it might be worthwhile to summarize for us and those who will be listening to this tape the nature of your work. What exactly does a ranger do?"

He scooted his chair a bit noisily. "Basically, my job was to help supervise the use of public property in this area. Our station was responsible for nearly two hundred thousand acres of land. As for specific tasks, they could be anything from overseeing the selling of timber to the planting of trees, release of wildlife, maintenance of trails, and planning of recreational activities."

He spread his hands, his face intent with the telling. "Needless to say, fire control was our big challenge and as part of that program, we also were responsible for supervising people hired on to assist us, like fire lookouts and smoke jumpers."

"Can you tell us how a ranger's life fits into the life of the communities they serve?" Billie asked, looking up from her legal pad where she'd jotted a few notes.

"The short answer is that they don't always fit, as I unfortunately found out."

"Sheeet! I feel another confession coming on," Stark chimed in, drawing a glare from Hatch.

Billie gritted her teeth. "Please go on, Mr. Hatch."

"Though a lot of the work was solitary stuff, traveling deep into the woods to carry out various chores, much of it also had to do with local landowners regarding land disputes."

"Can you give us an example?" She tapped her pen absentmindedly as she focused on the older man.

"Like they always were turning their pigs or cattle onto government land to graze, or starting unauthorized fires to kill off the ticks, or violating hunting regulations, or growing pot on forest lands." He leaned back in his chair, rubbing his chin in thought. "There was a whole list of illegal activities they were engaged in, but it all boiled down to the question of who controlled the land. As far as the locals were concerned, we were the interlopers."

"Interlopers? What does that mean?" Stark asked.

"Intruders," Billie volunteered. "Was this the majority view, Mr. Hatch?"

"No. No, not necessarily the majority view, but one strongly held by a determined minority. I don't mind telling you there was a palpable tension in the air at times. It was especially aggravating for someone like me who lived smack dab in one of the local communities." He brought his chair down with a thump.

"Which community?" she asked.

"Richfield, a town smaller than this one and also about forty miles from here. Some rangers live where they work, in ranger stations, far from the towns and cities."

"As long as I've lived here, I've never seen a ranger station. What are they like?" Mrs. Winfield asked, pausing to look up from the knitting in her hand.

"At the time I worked there, it was essentially a three-bedroom house with an attached garage. A couple of the residents added a chicken house to raise some poultry."

"Did you make special efforts to facilitate relations with local residents" Billie asked.

"Yes, I started a Friend of the Forest program–worked like hell to get it going, but it never took hold. I also helped draw up a Rails to Trails plan—"

"Rails to Trails? What's that?" she interrupted.

"It's when you turn abandoned railroad beds into hiking trails. It beats starting them from scratch and therefore a big money-saver."

Sounded like a great idea to her. "How did it work out?"

"It did some good, though it mainly appealed to the tourists, not the locals. Yeah, we were constantly being instructed on the importance of building bridges to the local communities. One ranger told me early on a good strategy was to befriend the local banker and make a point of going hunting or fishing with him." He lowered his voice slightly. "The idea was that most people in town owed him big time and were not about to make enemies with any close pals of his—"

"In other words, if the banker accepted you, so did the townspeople," she added.

"That was the deal. However, I didn't believe in playing games, which is what the situation around here became–a big game."

"How so?"

"The easiest way for angry locals to strike back at the government was–and still is, by the way–to drop a lighted match and walk away. Others would ignore warnings and continue with their own controlled burns. It became an ongoing battle for us to put out fires."

He drummed his fingers against the table, seemingly unaware of the sound. "They were like kids playing with matches, totally unconcerned with the potential danger. They mainly ended up being manageable brush fires, thanks to our efforts, I don't mind saying. I have come to the conclusion that people around here don't know what the big one is like. If they ever experienced one, maybe they'd be more careful."

"They need to watch more television," Stark suggested. "Pictures of those brush fires out west are on all the time."

"What's the big one, Mr. Hatch?" Billie asked.

"It's one that begins down in the debris and litter on the forest floor, the common brush fire. Usually, they cause little damage, unless they go undetected. If they're not detected, they can reach the dead wood and saplings, which act as a ladder for the flames to reach the treetops. Then you have the worst of all fires, the crown fire."

Hatch paused, seemingly for dramatic effect. "Temperatures in a crown fire can climb above fifteen hundred degrees, igniting the gases within the trees and exploding their tops. Depending on the wind, the flames can travel five to fifteen miles per hour or faster. You have to be damn quick to outrun them, that's for sure. A few years back, a fire crew got caught in a crown fire in Yellowstone Park. They were overrun and forced to take shelter in an abandoned mine shaft. Outside, the place felt like an oven. Inside, all of them soon fell unconscious from the combination of smoke and heat. When they were finally found, five of them were dead. The remainder had their boots and clothes nearly singed off."

"How horrible," Mrs. Winfield said softly, her hands completely stilled from her knitting.

"Yes, it is." Hatch's eyes flashed, reflecting the intensity burning within him like the conflagration he was describing.

"Imagine, if you can, a forest made up of wooden matchsticks as tall and as thick as the trees. That's the way I look at the forest, not as some playground where grown-ups can play with matches to no consequence. That's what it's become, I'm afraid, and like children, the grown-ups won't learn until their fingers feel the oven."

Released from the spell his words had cast, Billie realized that she might be violating every oral history procedural. First of all, what screening mechanism could she apply to authenticate what was being said? Yes, it was autobiographical, no question about that, and as with all autobiographies, doesn't the author, in shaping it, fictionalize it? Perhaps, this was history in its most raw form, unspoiled by interpretation, or was it, in fact, an interpretation?

Whatever, Mr. Hatch had a story to tell, full of scorn as it may be. Besides, who was she, a novice to the form and to the territory, to decide its worth?

"So, the burden grew?" she asked him.

"Yes, the drain on our workers became unbearable and I began to scream at my superiors that we needed to put a stop to the shenanigans and the only way to do it was to charge the perpetrators with a federal crime and take them to court. The government always was reluctant to do it, because they feared we would only upset the locals more. But finally we did it. We charged a guy with an illegal burn on federal property, and won the case. It definitely grabbed their attention. After that, the number of incidents decreased."

"And how did it affect their attitude toward the rangers?" Billie shifted uneasily in her chair.

"It hardened and became concentrated on me, since I was the main witness in the case. To make matters worse, while this was going on, I was getting pilloried by my own people."

"For what reason?"

His gaze shifted away from hers. "Headquarters sent down this regional supervisor to conduct an investigation. The guy spent a week going through our files and came up with a bunch of unsatisfactory items, mainly having to do with the number of fires."

"Why would they be blaming you for that?" Mrs. Winfield asked gently.

"Good question. It was not like we were the ones starting the fires."

"I thought you said the court case cut the number down?" Mr. Stark asked.

"It reduced them but not to the point where it satisfied the supervisor. The other problem we were facing was the one with the militia guys. They began to get in the game just about the time the court case was decided."

"Setting fires?" Billie leaned forward.

"Like I said, it's the easiest and quickest way to hit back at the government. They may or may not have been setting them, but they were contributing to the general unrest. What else are you going to do around here, bellyache to your congressman? Nothing gets people's attention like a fire."

"I would think many of the residents would be unhappy with their neighbors for setting fires, no matter how valid their complaints," Billie commented.

"You're right." He nodded to her. "Many were. But I'm talking about a determined minority who took it very personally. They were mostly non-townspeople–disgruntled farmers, hunters, crabby hillbillies."

"Sheeet, I hear you don't dare walk up and knock on the door of one of those hillbilly houses–that you should yell 'hello in there' from a safe distance, since they take a dim view of anyone talking to their wives while they're out of the house," Mr. Stark said.

"Wife, you mean," Billie corrected.

"Did I say wives?" he said, shaking with laughter, except Mr. Stark had one of those silent laughs where the whole torso would vibrate, but no sound would emit.

"Crabby is one way of describing them." Mr. Hatch leaned back in his chair. "Myself, I would add a few more adjectives."

"No wonder you retired," Billie said.

"It was a forced retirement." He cleared his throat roughly. "More like a firing. No, you haven't heard the worst of it."

"Then why the hell are you sticking around here?" Mr. Stark interrupted. "It sounds to me like you got enemies coming at you from all sides. If it was me, I'd have headed for the hills long ago."

"He is in the hills, Mr. Stark, and apparently this is not the end of his story, which we will continue next week. Perhaps, we will be able to squeeze yours in also," Billie said, bringing a smile to the cantankerous man's face.

Who knew? By the end of the workshops she might actually come to like the geezer.

"Do you think that's a good idea, Billie?" Shirley asked.

"Bringing my own computer into this office?" Billie glanced up at the volunteer who was now fast becoming her friend. "Probably not, but look at the stack of stuff piled on this desk I'll end up taking home to work on."

"What about a word processor? Would it help?"

"Now there's an option I doubt was addressed in any of the provisions of Mr. Whitington's will." She shuffled papers from one pile to another, organizing a filing system. "By the way, do you have any idea where I could put my hands on a copy of that document? I'd like to see the exact wording."

"I suppose the mayor might have one tucked away somewhere. Are you thinking the issue could be a bogus one?"

Shirley asked, passing her a stack of file folders.

"No. I believe it's real. However, I think it all centers on the card catalog. It's what he was seeking to preserve. He did not want an online catalog to replace it."

Billie looked up from the mess on her desk, thrusting her hands on her hip. "So, the question is how did he state his intentions in the wording? Did he state there would be no computers made available in the public service areas of the library? If that were the case, it would not apply to the non-public service areas, like our offices. Or, does it simply state the card catalog would remain in operation? In that case, the possibility exists the card catalog could remain in place side by side with an online one."

"Would the library continue to maintain the old catalog in that situation? Having two catalogs would lead to a lot of duplication and unnecessary maintenance costs, wouldn't it?"

"Yes, but you could freeze the card catalog, state to the public what the cutoff date is for it, and tell them if they wish to search for a more current title, they will need to use the online catalog. Meanwhile, the old catalog is still sitting there to ease their anxieties."

Shirley grinned. "Until they are weaned from it."

"Exactly," Billie said with an abrupt nod, though she doubted it would work out so simply. "It all depends on the wording in the will. If it says no computers in the library, we are left with little wiggle room."

"Other than sneaking one into your office."

"If I can't get a hold of a copy of the will, I just might end up doing that. At least it would force the issue."

"Speaking of the card catalog, I was planning on coming in for a couple of hours Sunday afternoon to catch up on some of my filing. The reason I'm telling you this is Scott overheard me mentioning it to Loretta and he immediately wanted to know if he could come in with me, so he could work on the books in the basement. My husband is going over to Poplar Bluff to play a round of golf with a buddy of his. He said he'd drop us off and pick us up."

"Fine with me." Billie chuckled. "And Scott, bless his heart. He is determined to find a diamond down there."

"Any chance of it?"

Billie rolled her eyes. "About the same chance as I have sneaking a computer in here without it being noticed."

Chapter Six

"Come on up–all you can see from there are horses' heads!"

Billie had exited her truck, expecting either him or Tripwire to make an appearance, when Cory called from the barn.

"Where's your guardian today?" she asked, cupping a hand over her eyes to shade them from a bright sun.

"He's around. You're old hat to him now," he said, untying the lead ropes from Houdini and another stallion with a spotted gray coat.

"What's his name?"

"Smoky Bottom."

She noticed other names–Brandy, Dead End, Dancer, burned in script below a succession of horseshoes nailed to the barn's interior. Mementos of other horses that had passed this way.

"Why does that horse have a red ribbon attached to its tail?" She pointed to a bay mare in a nearby stall, her nerves tingling with awareness as he stepped nearer.

"That tells you she's a kicker," he said, throwing a wry grin her way, "so you best know which end to approach her from, or else you may be setting yourself up for a sucker kick."

"I can't imagine how difficult it must be to take care of these horses by yourself."

"The owners who are boarding lend a hand, so it's not as difficult as it appears."

"I noticed your horse trailer outside. How often do you

have to take them on the road?"

"Often enough, usually to the vet or on a trail ride somewhere." He checked the saddle straps on her horse, tightening them a bit, before turning his attention back to her.

"Why would you go elsewhere?" She hoped her inquisitiveness indicated an interest rather than an ignorance.

"Oh, there are riding clubs all over the place, including some around here, that sponsor week-long trail rides. Now those are the ones that cause the horses some stress."

"In what way?"

"It separates them from their regular buddies. They're tied to a tree for longer periods. They're used to their own water. And just like people, the stress makes them sick, and gives them colic."

"And you more vet bills."

"Yeah, sometimes we'll do a little of the doctoring ourselves, like putting some electrolytes into their water, which makes it taste more like our water here. We'll also mix a little aspirin and bran into their feed. That can help. If not, it's off to the vet." He reached out to give Smokey Bottom an affectionate pat on the mane.

"What happens when you take them out on the highway and you have a breakdown, say a flat tire on the trailer?"

"First thing you do is make damn sure the horses don't get out on the highway, after you've unloaded them. Once you have them safely off to the side of the road, you get out your cowboy jacks and go to work fixing the tire."

"Cowboy jacks?" She was learning a whole new vocabulary.

"Yeah, you just back the trailer up on to them." He handed her the reins. "Ready?"

She took them and mounted the stallion, which moved not

a foot.

"Now, before we head out, Houdini has a small request to make," he said, holding on to her horse's bridle.

"Have you been talking to horses again?" she playfully asked.

"This one, I have."

"And what's his request?"

"He has this thing about show horses and their riders. You know, the kind you see on television at the big equestrian events where the horses have their manes all fancied up and the riders have their hair pinned back. Well, Houdini prefers it the other way," he continued, his eyes fixed on hers. "He'd like for you to let it flow like his."

She paused, before slowly and self-consciously reaching to the back of her head to remove a clasp, shaking her head to let loose her hair and with it, the notion that this might be a less dangerous ride.

Following him up the footpath, they coiled around the house where a small backyard garden came into view. At the moment, it was being tended by his grandparents who, upon noticing them, rose from their crouched positions to eagerly wave their greetings. Not the best of introductions, she conceded, in returning a wave, but one nonetheless.

Entering Shady Lane she clearly detected a rising energy level between the horses, as they bobbed and wove their necks, shuffled their feet side to side, and snorted their pleasure or displeasure at each other.

"Getting a little rambunctious, aren't they"? She attempted to settle the stallion with pats on the neck.

"They want to run," he replied, shifting his mount toward her.

"How do you know that?"

"Because I want them to. The energy is traveling from me to Smoky Bottom to Houdini to you. Feel it?"

"I feel something, but I'm not sure what."

"Grab the back of your saddle with your left hand, if you like, and hold on," he instructed, turning his horse to face her. "It's time to take off the training wheels."

She tightened her stomach, but nodded. "Okay."

"All set?"

"All set."

He reined his horse into a forward position alongside her and in the same instant gave it a kick that sent it bolting ahead. Houdini could not have reacted faster, if he'd been linked to Smoky Bottom by a two-foot towline. At once, necks were arched, manes flowing, nostrils flaring, flanks heaving, and hooves pounding as they charged down the lane. Occasionally, Cory would turn and flash her a reassuring smile, as if recognizing the passage she was going through.

It ended as it began, suddenly and feverishly, as the two horses pulled to a stop less than a length from where Shady Lance once met its own abrupt end.

"You can take your hand off the back of that saddle now." He turned his head from her, but not before she caught the grin splitting his face.

"Wasn't that a bit risky?" she asked, repeating the question her uncle undoubtedly would pose.

"It's risky when you have an inexperienced rider mounted on an inexperienced horse. We only have half of that equation."

"Is it true that you never become a real horseman until you are thrown from one?" she asked, watching the horses munching on some dried grass.

"Horse bit or horse thrown–there's some truth to it. It's

like taking that first tumble from a bike, or that first fastball in the back. Why?" He maneuvered his horse closer to hers. "You looking to earn your stripes by getting tossed?"

"No, but what's to prevent it?"

"Your horse not getting spooked."

"How do I avoid that?"

"There's not much you can do. It doesn't take a lot to panic them. Last year, we were out on a trail ride with this guy who was on this Appaloosa he was boarding. It began to rain, so one of his buddies tossed him a rain slicker, which spooked the horse no end." He redirected his gaze from the trail to her. "The mount ended up trying to climb a tree with him still on it. He finally got bucked, before the horse settled down."

"Was he injured?"

"The horse?"

"No! The rider," she shouted, leaning over to tap his thigh.

He laughed. "No broken bones, which is about the best a thrown rider can hope for. Believe it or not, he was lucky the horse was trying to climb the tree rather than skirt it."

"Lucky?"

"The most dangerous things around when a horse panics are tree limbs. A spooked horse will take a run at anything and if he's headed through a forest, chances are his rider is going to be neck-tied by a limb."

"Has it happened to you?"

"Yes, but I managed to grab hold of the first limb I passed under, which was the smartest dismount I've ever made."

He tugged his horse away from the brush and guided it to a path leading up a narrow incline.

"Let's go," he said. "This time we're headed up instead of down."

She trailed him to the top where the path leveled off and began a parallel route to the river below. The woods were mostly behind and below them, replaced by a series of steep bluffs with broad rock surfaces.

"Not to denigrate Florence, but I think you look much better on Smoky Bottom," she called ahead, breaking a lengthy silence.

She received no answer. She tried again, believing the stiff breeze sweeping across the bluff may have muted her message.

"So," he responded, holding his attention to the trail, as if he considered the remark an insult to Florence, after all.

So? So I only meant it as a compliment, she thought to herself, as they settled into another period of silence, which held until their arrival at a cliff overlook.

"We'll stop here." He reined his horse in. "It's a favorite spot of mine."

They hitched their horses to the stems of a bush and took a seat on a rock ledge skirting the edge of the cliff.

"I can see why." She surveyed the sight, soaking in the tranquil beauty.

"You won't be able to pinpoint them because of the trees," he said, nudging her arm, "but right below us are the bat cave and sections of river we crossed last week, and further on down is Woodland Hills."

He was right. She could identify little but a sea of trees and the sliver of a river winding through them.

"What's that over there?" she asked, pointing to something that she could see, a complex of buildings nestled in the middle of a clearing.

"That?" His gaze followed her outstretched finger.

"Yes."

"That's the monks' place."

"The monks' place?" She jerked her head around. Now he'd really surprised her. "You mean a monastery?"

"If that's what they call a monks' place, though I've always thought of a monastery as looking like a big fort with tall walls and observation posts surrounding it, like one of those medieval castles."

She grinned. "And a moat and drawbridge."

"Yeah, something like that." He shrugged. "I guess the monks had to defend themselves against enemies too, like vandals or pirates. They make fruitcakes down there, good ones, I hear, if you like fruitcakes."

"How interesting. How do you get to the complex?"

He clasped her arm and turned her attention off to the right. "There's an access road. It's the next one past the road leading to my place. You know, I have a hard time imaging a fruitcake operation down there."

"You mean, like conveyer belts carrying the fruitcakes along, while the monks scramble to try and box them?" Her arm felt warm where he still held it.

"Something like that."

"A twenty-four-hour-a-day operation, you think?"

"Wouldn't surprise me. I hear they're always up."

She restrained a smile. "I'm sure they set aside some time for devotional duties."

"You Catholic?"

"Yes."

"How come?"

"How come?" She laughed. "Oh, I guess I've always loved a good mystery. What about you?"

"We got all kinds to choose from around here—of the Protestant variety, I mean. I usually end up with my grandparents at a small Baptist church down the way."

"You must feel like you're living out a dream here."

"Dreams are for chasing, not for having."

"Are you chasing one?"

"No," he said, looking into the beyond. "At least not like the guy who was traveling through here a while back. This guy came driving up to my barn one morning in a converted school bus he'd driven all the way from Florida. It was full of these exotic birds he'd brought with him."

"Exotic birds?"

"That's right. Parrots, parakeets, macaws, or whatever you call them. He was a retired rent-a-cop who'd taken out all of his savings to buy those birds."

"What in the world for?"

"He was on his way to Oklahoma. Said he was taking them to some reservations to sell to the Indians. Some guy told him they had all kinds of government money to spend and were crazy for exotic birds. He claimed he could sell them for ten times the purchase price. Since he'd paid $50,000 for the whole bunch, he figured he would be pocketing about a half million bucks."

Her eyes widened. "What was he doing here?"

"Wanting to know if there were any reservations in this area that he might check out. I told him no, but I did let him remove all those birdcages off his bus and wash them down with my hose." He wagged his head and let out a low whistle. "You should have heard the racket. Every loud birdcall you could imagine was ricocheting through the trees. My cats went crazy. Anyway, there was one guy who was following a dream. How about you, you chasing one?" he asked, lowering the levity.

She thought a moment before answering. "Nothing as

exotic as your Florida friend had in mind. Most of my dreams are of the nighttime variety and usually have to do with the past and me in the middle of it. I don't as easily envision myself in the future."

"You never think of what you'd like to be doing down the road?"

"Yes, but I always considered that more of vision than a dream. I often have pictured myself as a leading rare book dealer or appraiser, traveling the world, and getting paid for my opinions."

She turned her gaze to the surrounding scenery. "On the other hand, I've seen myself as a wife and mother, settled in some pleasant little neighborhood, making everyone around me happy. Come to think of it, maybe it is more of a dream than a vision."

"I had what you might call a vision the other night," he said.

"Oh, of what?"

"Of you down there on the bank of the river, after our crossing," he said, motioning down the hillside.

She recalled the moment with the rush of the experience. "Is that so?"

"Yes. It reminded me of something Captain Jack was supposed to have said, while he was watching a young Indian maiden bathing in the river."

"Watching from behind a tree?" She smirked.

"Could have been from behind a tree or from the bank. Who knows?"

"What was it he said?"

Slowly and nervously he plucked from his back pocket a crumpled slip of paper and began to read in a tone both unaffected and engaging.

"Behold your bawdy beads
Pursuing paths of pleasure flee
Over fragrant fields of flesh to end,
Vanished by an envious wind."

"Those lines came from Captain Jack?"

She couldn't restrain her note of surprise.

"Like I said–supposedly," he responded, slipping the paper back into his pocket.

"It was the Jacks Fork's bawdy beads he was speaking of?"

"Yes, except it wasn't known as the Jacks Fork then."

"But it was Captain Jack who was doing the beholding?"

"Yes, or at least that's the story. I read an article in a newsletter put out by a local historical group claiming the lines were his."

"And you put them to paper?"

"I did the other night when that vision came to me. I still had the newsletter lying around, so I looked it up again." His nervousness seemed to recede the deeper he went into his explanation. "However, I don't think it was Captain Jack who spoke those words. He may have said something close to them, but then they were probably prettied up later on by someone else, especially since it's doubtful he talked much English in the first place."

"You're thinking something was lost or added in the interpretation or translation," she suggested.

"Yeah, I figure ol' Jack was speaking in sign language. I don't imagine he was scribbling the words down on a piece of paper. More than likely, he was talking to his buddies about the river and the wind having their way with the girl.

Somebody then picked up on it and somewhere down the line, somebody else put it on paper. That's where the something was lost or added."

She felt pleased by his perception, his understanding. "I understand Native Americans often attach human qualities to the land's natural features. It has a way of adding a romantic element to the language. Those unique qualities are not easily translated into English, particularly in such an alliterative manner."

"Whatever. All I know is whoever said it was just another guy having a vision, like I had of you," he said, a smile coming to his face. "So, a traveling book dealer; does that mean you consider books your companions?"

"Interesting you should say that." She sighed, glad to be back on a more familiar topic. "It's what we try and teach the children who come into the library, to look at books as their companions. They will make you laugh, make you cry, and make you think. Take them to bed and they may even put you to sleep."

"Not a bad thing for adults."

"Which is why we spread the message at an early age."

"Well, I wish I could say the same about my companions," he said, motioning to the horses. "They seldom make me laugh or cry, much less put me to sleep out on the trail. Come to think of it, next time it might not be a bad idea for you to bring along a book, maybe sit and read, while I do the watching."

"No, as much as I cling to them, I would be the first to admit they are no substitute for the flesh-and-blood kind of companion."

"The kind that can touch your body as well as your mind," he observed, fixing his eyes on her.

She gulped. "Yes, I guess you could say that. Is this your

private space here, your getaway place?" she asked, stirring to his presence.

"It is today." He moved with confidence, taking her hand in his and stroking it gently.

For the first time in a long while, she no longer felt alone.

He found her lips behind a lock of windblown hair, exploring and exciting them with his own, awakening in her a passion already primed in anticipation of his kiss. Yes, she was ready to be touched by flesh and blood and gladly gave her own in return.

"Time to go," he unexpectedly whispered, opening her eyes to his.

She followed him to the horses, suddenly grateful for his reserve, and a decision she didn't have to make.

"Do we continue on the same path?" she asked, realizing too late the untimely wording.

"We can't." He chuckled, confirming the faux pas. "The government won't allow it."

"The government won't allow it?" she responded, trying to stifle a giggle.

"The trail leads through public land further on down. They cut off the access."

"Why?"

"They have their reasons—reasons others might not agree with."

They doubled back on the trail they traveled up on, repeating the full gallop down Shady Lane, this time with her hand free of the saddle.

It had been an exhilarating ride. One she would never forget. Not in the least because of the man who rode by her side, leading her to new adventures.

What wasn't repeated was his offer for her to return the

following week, causing her a moment of anxiety. Until he asked for her phone number, a request she readily granted.

What to make of it? What to make of him? What must he be making of her? The questions dominated and delighted her on her return home, blinded her to matters of the library, to the access road she was traveling—*to the tree limb that had fallen across it.*

She hit the brakes, but not before she crossed it, only then realizing it was not a limb but a living thing. She peered into the rearview mirror at the coiling snake in the middle of the road. Was it injured?

She recalled someone saying that running over a snake caused it no harm. It did manage to coil itself into a big lump, after all. She and the snake appeared frozen in place, neither willing to make the first move. Finally, she edged her truck forward, five, ten, fifteen yards before the snake uncoiled and wiggled into the underbrush. She exhaled, scanned the road ahead to see if it was clear, and weighed down on the accelerator.

She needed to see a deer. At least one thing around here should fit her image of forest charm.

"It was nothin' but a big old black snake," her uncle said.

"It was huge," she said in exasperation, stretching her hands wide.

"Yeah, they can get up to six feet long." He waved his fork absentmindedly. "Farmers like 'em. They eat the rats and other rodents. They also climb trees to feed on birds and their eggs."

"Please, Uncle Ray, not over dinner. I just hope I didn't hurt it."

"You must have missed its head, so it should be okay," he

said, munching on a piece of fried chicken he'd cooked up for the two of them.

"Are they poisonous?" She shuddered with belated reaction.

"No, their bite's harmless, but don't tell Buster that. He got bit by one when he put his nose into the wrong place."

"I had a nice time today." She shifted the subject.

"You already told me that. What's this guy's name again who runs the place?"

"Cory. Cory Winslow." Just saying his name started the stirrings inside.

"Can't say I know him. From the way you've been describin' things though, I think you may be takin' more of an interest in him than his horses."

"He does have these nice hazel eyes," she said, feeling a twinkle in her own.

"Here I am, an ol' single guy, settled down in the wilderness, with no great worries and responsibilities, and now look what happens."

"Come on, Uncle Ray, you know you like having me around." She patted his arm with affection...and reassurance. "Besides, I can take care of myself."

"What do you have in common with this guy?"

"We both like animals."

"You mean certain kinds of animals."

"Well, yes."

"Anything else?"

"Mountain air."

"These aren't mountains, they're hills."

"Okay, hill air."

"Can I tell you something you don't have in common?" he asked, pointing his fork at her.

Her curiosity was tweaked. "Of course."

"You're smarter than he is."

"What makes you think that?" she asked, surprised at the statement.

"Because you're smarter than just about anyone in this town. You have the schoolin'."

"So, it's where I am that makes me smarter, you seem to be saying. Well, suppose I'm traveling through the wilderness on a horse with him–on separate horses, I should say. Who then is the smarter, taking into consideration where we are?"

"You."

"*Aaaarrgghh!*"

"I bet if you asked that Cory fellow the same question out on the trail, he would have given you the same answer."

"Maybe, because he's considerate. And since when does smarter necessarily make someone better, or for that matter, right? When people begin to believe they're smarter, they begin to place themselves above others. That's when trouble begins to brew." She rose to take her empty plate to the sink in a feeble effort to end the conversation.

"I'm the one placing you above others. The way I see it, he likes horses, you like horses and books." His words trailed her into the kitchen.

"Is it that simple? Listen, I've been introduced to many a smart guy in my life. Give me the one with common sense any day. Haven't you heard? A little learning is a dangerous thing."

"So's a little stupidity."

"I repeat. I had a nice day."

"Sorry, didn't mean to put a damper on your day. If anyone deserved a good one, it's you."

"No, no, you haven't." She returned to the table to grab

more dishes. "I know you mean well."

"To tell you the truth, what you were sayin' about the militia guys asking to use your meeting room gives me more concern than this Cory fellow. And, like you said, his likin' animals–it does count."

"On the subject of animals, is there a zoo around here?" she asked.

"A zoo? The closest one is probably over in Springfield. The only other one I can think of is a petting zoo they have over in Brookfield. Why?"

"Do they have deer?"

"Deer?" he repeated. "They're all over the place. Why do you need to go to a zoo to see one?"

"They're hiding from me."

"Oh, I see," he purled, as if wanting to reel back his "you're smarter" opinion.

Chapter Seven

Woodland Hills was a pleasant enough name for the community, a bit suburban sounding to her, but nonetheless fitting. Still, Billie was on the verge of believing a more appropriate moniker might have been 'Tween' Town.

For the third time since she'd taken the job, a salesman was sitting in her office, relating how he happened to be on his way from St. Louis to Springfield, when he decided on the spur of the moment to drop in to introduce himself and his products. Possibly, it was the good mood she was in coming off an enjoyable weekend that led her to listen patiently to his pitch, presented with all the pace and spirit of a practiced preacher.

The problem was with his products–a line of CD-ROM reference resources. The astonished look on his face, when she finally had to inform him of the library's no-computer status, was an understandable one. To ease his dismay, she advised him of the chance the library soon would be providing computer access and that she'd be pleased to keep his product line under consideration. On that note he handed her a pile of brochures and left.

"Are you free?" Shirley asked, popping her head through the door.

"Yes, what's up?"

"I wanted to let you know the militia people are in the meeting room."

Billie jerked upright. "How many of them are there?"

"Twenty or thirty, I'd say."

"Everyone behaving themselves?"

"As far as I know." Shirley shrugged. "There have been no complaints. They're not in uniform, which helps, though I can't help feeling a little tension in the air. Here's the application," she said, handing it over for Billie's perusal.

"There's no signature! Tell them their leader needs to sign it before they leave." She placed the form on her desk.

"I'll inform them the minute their meeting breaks up." Shirley paused, waiting until she had Billie's attention again. "Have you seen the basement?"

"No. I was just going down to take a quick look. How did it go Sunday?"

"We were here for about three hours. From what I could tell, it looked like Scott worked his way through a ton of those boxes."

"I'm sure he'll feed me all the details this afternoon." She grinned in anticipation. "It'll be nice to get that place cleaned out. The more I think about it, the more I like the idea of converting it into a historical museum."

"I also wanted to tell you our rope has been stolen."

"The display rope?"

Shirley nodded. "Yes, one of the patrons noticed it missing this morning."

"And we don't know who took it, I presume." She sighed. Always something...

"No. I hope we don't find anyone hanging from it. Should we report it to the sheriff's office?"

"I don't think it's of enough value to worry about. It is one more reason to have a separate space for a museum, however."

"Okay, I'd better head back to the desk."

"Be sure and remind the militia guys about the application. It will be waiting for them right here," she called after Shirley, nodding to the form.

"Do you want me to get the signature?"

"No. Let them sign it here. They're probably going to ask for permission to book it next month. Is that date open, by the way?"

"Yes."

"I was thinking," Billie said, tapping her pencil against her bottom lip, "wouldn't that be a fine time to hold our staff meetings, the first Monday of each month at ten o'clock?"

"Monday mornings are always a good time for staff meetings," Shirley concurred with a smile.

"Book it."

"Yes ma'am, right away."

Billie counted a dozen boxes of books remaining in the basement. Shirley was right. Scott did have a very productive day. She took time to spot check some of his work, noting some of the additional points she'd need to bring to his attention.

Satisfied they would be able to finish that afternoon, she returned to her office to poke through her file cabinets. She was hoping to unearth either a report or piece of correspondence that could provide further insight into what Mr. Whitington's specific intent was in regard to the library's future direction. It wasn't as though she expected to discover a copy of his final will. Yet, neither was it unreasonable to think a document or unofficial memo filed away somewhere might lend a clue.

She'd burrowed to the bottom drawer of the file cabinet, when she heard the familiar voice behind her.

"Houdini said to say hello."

"Cory, what a surprise!" she exclaimed, losing all thoughts

of Mr. Whitington, as she rose to greet him.

"I wasn't sure you'd recognize me without a horse nearby."

"I could say the same thing about me without my jeans on," she countered, gesturing to herself.

He looked her over, his grin appreciative. "You look nice."

"Thank you. Well, what brings you this way?" she asked, hoping it was her, but speculating it could be one of those between-town stops.

"I understand I'm supposed to sign something."

"Sign something?"

"A meeting-room application form."

Him? Cory? A member of the militia?

"Application form–application form–let's see–" She strove mightily to maintain her composure. Wasn't that what a manager did in crisis situations? A heart and mind were colliding in the workplace–her heart and mind and her workplace–and now she was expected to separate the personal from the professional?

"Is this what you are referring to?" she said, handing him the application while avoiding his eyes.

"Is there a problem, Billie?" he asked straightforwardly, signing the form and handing it back.

She noted he'd added the title "President" behind his name. There was no disguising her concern, no false pretenses to hide behind, no avoiding the collision.

"Do you have time to talk?" she asked, motioning to a chair.

"Sure," he said, apparently oblivious to the specifics of her concern.

"Cory, what exactly is the purpose of your organization, if you don't mind me asking?"

"Our purpose?" He spread his hands. "To defend a way of life, our property. Yeah, that's how I'd put it."

"Against whom?"

"The federal government." He shifted in his chair, his eyes taking on a guarded look. "Why is this of concern to you?"

"Because I don't believe in violence."

"Who says we are violent? Believe me, we'd love to find a solution other than going to war."

"Granted, I'm not an authority on this, but from what I've been reading, militia groups are military-type entities. They hold battlefield exercises in the woods." She gripped her pen tighter, holding her disappointment inside. "They train with guns. They stockpile weapons. They publish books, manuals, and videos on how to conduct guerilla warfare–and so on."

"So does the U.S. Army."

"But they are a legal entity."

"And so are we. We're not a violent organization. We're not into driving tanks into burning buildings with babies trapped inside them."

Lips that not long ago were caressing hers were now contesting her, she observed with whimsical attention.

"It's about our land and who controls it, Billie," he continued. "In case you weren't aware, it belongs to us, like a child to its parents," he added, jabbing his chest with a forefinger. "That's all we've got. Take that away from us and we're left with nothing."

"How is it being taken away?"

"Piece by piece, through purse strings and intimidation. They're not like an army that marches onto your property in broad daylight and claims it. The bureaucrats are more clever than that. No, they first create a dependency on them with their offers of financial help. Then they start saying if you don't do this or that with the money, we will take it back, or they'll buy up the property all around you and isolate you."

She leaned her head closer to his. "The government is us, Cory. We make of it what we will. If you don't approve of what your representatives are doing, then vote somebody else in."

"I'm talking about the federal bureaucracy. There is no changing it whether you vote someone new in or not. It's too late for that." He leaned back and breathed a sigh of disgust. "Like I said, they're not like an army marching in full view, but you know what? In the end it's what they will have to do to take complete control and that's what we mean to prevent."

For the most part, he was calm in making his case. Was it for lack of conviction or a conviction he was right? She wanted to remind him of where they were—in the middle of a library, not in the middle of the wilds. Here, he was no longer the smart one. That's what she wanted to tell him, but the images of horses in full gallop, trees stretching to the sky, cliffs rising, a river flowing, and a kiss kept getting in the way.

"Was it you who planned on using our meeting room all along?"

"No, I was informed Saturday evening it was available to us."

She arched a brow. "Don't you find it a little ironic that you are utilizing a government facility to conduct your meetings?"

He pursed his lips, shaking his head. "Our beef is with the federal government, not with the locals. Do you receive federal funds?"

"In an indirect way, yes," she replied, sensing where he was heading. "As a matter of fact, we are a public library operating almost exclusively on private funds."

"And you expect it to last?"

"If the strings attached to the private funds don't isolate us."

"And if they do?"

"Then we'll follow an alternative course."

He flashed that disarming smile of his, as if he'd made a point.

Over his shoulder she noticed a man pacing the hallway, glancing inside her office each time he passed the doorway. "One of your friends is waiting for you."

"Yes, I know. I'd like to book the meeting room for next month," he said confidently.

"It's already booked," she answered instantly.

"I see." His eyes flickered briefly with anger…and hurt.

Message sent and received.

"You know, our meeting here has nothing to do with the library, Billie. Ours is not a library program."

"But it does reflect on us, Cory." She stared at the pen clasped tightly in her hand. "It may not be sponsored by us, but people associate what takes place in the library with the library."

"Even though we've broken no rules?"

"The ultimate decision on use of the meeting room resides with me. Whether rules are observed or not is only one of the factors taken into consideration."

"Hmm. Doesn't quite sound fair to me, but hey, you're the boss," he said, rising from the chair. "Nice seeing you again, Billie," he added, his long face marking his confusion on his way out the door.

She watched him casually stroll out of her office, utter something to his cohort, and leave.

"No offense, nothing personal, everything professional," she whispered to an empty chair, closing her eyes to shut out the moment.

"You didn't buckle, did you?" Shirley asked from the doorway.

"No, I didn't buckle," she answered in a detached tone, forcing her attention on the papers cluttering her desk.

"I didn't think you would. Going home for lunch?"

"No, I brought along a snack today. I think I'll just sit in my office and have it here." Alone. With time to think.

"Are you okay?"

"I'm fine." She stood and turned her back, walking to a file cabinet to feign a search for a folder.

"Scott's down in the basement. I told him you'd probably be down in a while," Shirley said, plainly oblivious to the tension still filling the air.

"Thanks. I'm heading there shortly." Her spirits lifted just a mite. There was an outside chance Scott might be able to nip her budding melancholy with his enthusiastic inquisitiveness.

He'd winnowed the boxes down to a final one by the time she joined him.

"Sorry, Scott, I seem to have let you do all the dirty work."

"Oh, that's okay Miss Staley, I've enjoyed this," he said, as he ripped open the last container.

She examined his work and once more made only minor adjustments from the book-sale pile to the possible library addition stack.

"What exactly is a first edition?" he asked, hauling an armful of books to the book-sale pile. "Does that mean the first copies to come out?"

"To be precise, it means those copies of books printed from the first typesetting."

"That's why reprints and second or later editions don't count?"

"Don't count to collectors generally speaking. Remember what I said about old not necessarily meaning rare?" Things weren't always what one hoped them to be. A fact she'd do well to remember.

"Yes," Scott answered, drawing back her attention.

"The same holds true for first editions. The term doesn't equate to rare. The fact is most books have only one edition."

They promptly dispatched the final box and sat back to admire the before and after.

"Good job, Scott. When these get laid out on tables for the book sale, I'll scan them again to see if we missed anything of note. The good news is we have plenty here for a book sale. And speaking of that, how would like to help with it?"

"Sure. I did want to ask you about a couple of books I set aside," he said, reaching under his chair to retrieve them, unable to disguise the expectation in his eyes. "One is this book on restoring cars. In case you don't know, I'm really into old cars and I'd love having this book."

"No problem, take it. Maybe some day you'll be into old books like you are into old cars."

"And this is one I'd like to have to send to my sister," he said, handing it to her.

Her eyes immediately were drawn to the title, *A Good Man Is Hard to Find* and the author, Flannery O'Connor. Carefully, she browsed through the pages, noting in particular the title page and its verso.

"Oh, Scott, you're a dandy for helping with this project, but this is one book I can't let you have." She looked at him, apology lodged in her eyes.

"Well, that's okay." He shrugged. "Like I said, I was only

going to send it to my older sister in Kansas City. She's always complaining there are no good men up there, so I thought this might give her some tips on finding one."

"I don't think the kind of man Miss O'Connor writes about is the kind you want hanging around your sister," she said, trying to contain her mirth. "No, this book is going into our bookcase upstairs."

"Really?" His eyes widened instantly. "That one?"

"This book is a first edition, Scott." She paused to enjoy his reaction.

He jumped from his chair, examining the book over her shoulder, something she would have done given the same circumstance.

"Look at its condition. It's nearly immaculate, including the dust jacket, and to top it off, it's signed by the author. I would guess the previous owner of the book may have lived in Georgia at one time and attended one of her signings."

"It's just a collection of short stories, isn't it? Do they have much value?"

"They do when they come from her hand."

She held the book against a narrow beam of sunlight slicing through the slit of a basement window and again contemplated the title. Unable to contain the bubble of mirth rising within her, she let go with a giggle followed by a hearty laugh.

"What's so funny, Miss Staley," he inquired. "Is it a comedy?"

"It's a tragic comedy," she replied.

"What's that?"

"It means you don't know whether to laugh or cry," she replied, cutting loose with another round of laughter that continued uninterrupted.

She could see him wondering whether they were tears of sorrow or laughter welling in her eyes, a question she herself could not answer.

"Come on. Let's take this book upstairs. I'll let you do the honors of putting it in the bookcase," she said, gaining some self-control. "I'll also buy you your own copy, not a first edition of course, so you can send it to your sister. Maybe she can learn a lesson about men from it after all."

And maybe I can too.

Billie had planned on broaching her uncle on the Cory episode after dinner, but he was feeling under the weather and decided to turn in early. Instead, she chose to spend the evening browsing the Internet for information on militias. In the course of her search, she was amazed to find the scores of web sites devoted to the movement.

Despite the variety, the sites featured common topics, such as the New World Order, gun rights, gun shows, and U.S. constitutional guarantees. Most sites also had schedules for martial arts and firearms training exercises, as well as reviews of outdoor equipment and essays on survival techniques.

At one stage she interrupted her search to listen to the sound of distant voices, which gradually faded. If they were disconcerting before, they were more so now, since she was able to put a face on them.

Her eyes grew weary following the flickering computer images. She was winding down and realized she only had enough attentiveness left to conduct a search on public libraries and militia groups to determine if the meeting-room issue she faced had been confronted by others.

A rap outside on the cabin door brought her pecking on the keyboard to a halt, momentarily freezing her movements.

Who could that be? Her uncle would have called out her name.

"Who's there?" she called.

No answer.

She glanced at the window but saw no movement. Unfortunately, the cabin was built long before safety features became standard fare. She was afforded no full view of the porch from the window, nor was there a peephole in the door to observe the entranceway.

"Uncle Ray, is that you?"

Again, no answer. But for the low hum of the computer, quiet had returned. She considered dialing her uncle but did not wish to wake him for the sole reason of her being a wimp. After all, this was rural America, not a crime-infested city street.

She dialed anyway, despite her reluctance. No answer. What if he'd been hurt? Perhaps he needed help.

She edged the front door open and stepped onto an empty porch. Slowly, she descended the steps to the footpath leading to the cabin. The lights in her uncle's house were out.

By now, Buster would have been at her heels, but he often slept at his master's bedside when they were both in need of company. It must have been a chance occurrence of some kind, perhaps a raccoon scrambling across her porch. She turned back to her cabin.

"Hello, Miss Staley," the thick voice said.

One of the militia. The sleepy-eyed one, standing equal distance with her from the front porch, having stepped from the side of the cabin, she presumed.

"What do you want?" she asked, fixing her eyes on the man she'd last seen in the library parking lot.

"I just wanted to let you know, no hard feelings about the

other day."

"How did you find me?" Her fingernails bit into the palms of her clenched hands.

"I'm very familiar with your truck. It's an easy one to spot."

"Okay, no hard feelings. Now, I think you had better leave," she said, wishing she had changed from her nightshirt, before she'd left the cabin.

"As a friendly gesture, I'd thought you'd like to take a walk down to our camp site." His eyes shifted slightly. "I'll show you there's no reason to be concerned about us."

"Did Cory Winslow send you?"

"Cory? No, are you a friend of his?"

"Yes," she said, realizing he was unaware of any relationship.

"Funny, he's never mentioned your name, though he doesn't have much to say to me, anyway."

"Is he with you?"

"No, he's not here tonight. Had some other business to take care of. The camp's all emptied out now, so it would be a good time to let me show you around."

"I'm not exactly dressed for it. Why don't I go in and change. It'll only take a—"

"No, I think you're dressed just right for it." His gaze crawled over her. The animal in him had taken over–as if there could be some other force of nature within him.

Billie hurriedly considered her options. The last thing she was going to do was head into the woods with him. She could sprint for the trees but that would be like running into his lair. Sprinting to her cabin was also out of the question. He had the angle on her. Her only other option was to scream, something she never recalled doing since childhood. She considered it a sign of weakness–nobody would make her scream. Besides, he had a hunting knife attached to his belt and a look in his eye that augured he would kill anything or anyone that got between him and his prey.

"So, why don't we take that little walk," he hissed.

"I think you had better leave," she repeated, attempting to conceal any indication of the fear rising within her.

He took the first step toward her.

A twig cracked behind her.

"I think you had better leave, like she said," her uncle's voice snapped from the garden.

It was enough to momentarily halt him, as he cast a glance to her uncle and then back to her.

"And who might you be, her father?" he said, keeping his gaze on her.

"Father–uncle–brother–husband, what does it matter?"

"Oh, it matters, because if I was any one of those you mentioned, I sure wouldn't be allowing her to sleep in a separate bed."

She'd never seen her uncle angry, but the seeds were swelling within him. His chest heaved. It was now a male thing and she feared for him.

Each was poised for the next move that would unleash the fury, except it came from neither, for, suddenly, came the deepest, sweetest, guttural growl she'd ever heard. The lab was crouched in the shadows aside her, inching his way forward, head low to the ground, nose locked onto a scent, teeth glistening in the night.

Perhaps it was the animal-to-animal talk that led the sleepy-eyed one to blink.

"Like I said, Miss Staley, no hard feelings."

He turned but hesitated, as if to launch one more parting

shot, before melting back into the darkness.

"I thought you said Buster wasn't a good guard dog!" She fondled the animal's head.

Her uncle stepped aside her. "I didn't know he had it in him."

"You did so," she teased, able to breathe a bit easier now that the danger had passed.

He jerked his hand toward the wood. "You know that guy?"

"He was one of the militia people in the parking lot I was telling you about."

"I'm goin' to call Dan Booker in the morning."

"The sheriff?"

"Yeah, he's a good man. He needs to know about this." He removed his cap and wiped sweat from his forehead with the back of his hand. "You should have called me."

She straightened her spine.

"I can take care of myself."

"I'm going back to bed. The dog stays with you."

"Uncle Ray, he just knocks things over. The last time I let him in—"

"*The dog stays with you*," he said, cutting her off.

"Okay, okay." Obviously this was not the time to cross him.

He only knocked over a cup before she got him settled at the foot of her bed. It took a while longer to settle herself and for her mind to return to Cory. There was nothing like an attempted assault to refocus one's attention.

But the question remained. What was she to do?

Chapter Eight

"Billie, you're wanted in the meeting room."

"Now what?"

"I'm not sure," Shirley said, assuming her usual stance in Billie's doorway. "Loretta called down and told me they needed you up there for something."

Billie dropped the envelope she'd been opening, the letter-opener clattering on her desk. "It's not a militia issue, tell me that, Shirley."

"I don't know," she said, glancing away.

Billie debated on the way up whether it was a wise idea at all for a library to have a meeting room for public use. From past memos she'd been reading, it appeared to be the epicenter of conflict. Questions of who was and who wasn't eligible to use it led the problem list, followed by the bans on food and fund-raising in the room. But then, it was an integral part of the public library's mission, more so in a small town like Woodland Hills where it was regarded as the hub of community social activity.

Braced for the worse case scenario, she swung open the door and stepped into a musical salute.

"*Happy birthday to you—*"

Scott, Loretta, and kids from Loretta's story hour session were standing around a table adorned with red, white, and blue bunting and balloons. A chocolate cake, sprouting lit candles, served as the centerpiece.

"*Happy birthday, dear Billie, happy birthday to you.*"

"Okay, who squealed?" she asked, hands on hips, not quite recovered from the surprise.

"It was me. I'm the official birthday tracker," Shirley confessed, arriving behind her.

Billie blew out the candles in a single breath and accepted her gift. Nicely wrapped, but there was no disguising its contents. She had handled too many books in her lifetime to not have divined what was inside. She tossed to the side the shredded wrapping and held aloft the title–*Libraries and Computers: Which Way the Revolution?*

"We'll soon find out," she laughed.

"Is that one going into the case, Miss Staley?" Scott asked.

"I don't think *soooo*," she drawled. "And why aren't you at school this morning?"

"Teachers Day," he replied. His freckles wrinkled when he grinned.

She thanked them and stayed for the cake and Loretta's story hour. Afterwards, she returned to her office to finish going through files, finding no additional evidence of Mr. Whitington's intentions.

The remainder of the day she spent at the circulation desk waiting on patrons and in her office reviewing oral history tapes. The next session might well be the final one, if Mr. Hatch's portion could be completed in short order and if Mr. Stark's session, with a little prompting from her, could be wrapped up as well, though she could only imagine the tale he might spin.

"I spoke with Dan Booker this morning," her uncle said.

As had become a nightly ritual, they were relaxing after dinner on the patio.

"What did he say?" Billie asked, sipping on her tea.

"That he would take care of it. He knows who the guy is. Says there's a warrant out for his arrest and is planning on picking him up."

"Warrant for what? Did he say?"

"Assault and battery on an ex-girlfriend." He stared at her fixedly, as if still blaming her for going out of her cabin alone.

She flinched. "I can't imagine anyone being his girlfriend."

"Booker has five daughters. He'll take care of it." He paused to pat Buster on the head. "So, this Cory fellow is their leader, you were tellin' me."

"Yes."

"That must have come as a shock."

"To say the least. I just don't understand it. He seemed like the classic country gentleman and now to learn he's associated with a degenerate like that guy."

He arched a brow. "Do you think he's aware of what went on last night?"

"Cory?" She shook her head slowly, her stomach knotting at his name. "I don't think so. I sure hope not."

"He hasn't tried calling you?"

"No," she said, still vacillating between whether she wanted him to or not.

"Well, on the one hand I think it can be a mistake to lump people all together," her uncle said. "There may be some okay fellows in those militia groups. Just because someone is angry with the government, doesn't necessarily make him a bad guy. Plenty of people are angry with the government. On the other hand, who they pal around with can tell you something."

"Like their lack of judgment."

"It sounds to me like you're already starting to sour on the men around here."

"I'll have you know, I've met some nice men here."

"Like who?"

"Oh, let's see…uh…uh…" Billie began to giggle.

"You can't name one." He interrupted her mirth.

"Oh, yes I can. Scott."

He cut her a glance from under his eyebrows. "Isn't he that boy who does volunteer work?"

"Yes, and a very nice one. Also a very cute one, I might add."

"How old is he?"

"Seventeen or so."

"Let's see…if you hang around 'till he's about thirty, that would make you thirty-eight or so." He nodded his head slowly, his eyes twinkling at her. "That's not so bad. It would give him plenty of time to do some courtin'."

"Yes, he could help me sort books for the next dozen years, forgoing whatever career ambitions he might have in mind," she cracked. "In time we could chuck this older sister, younger brother thing we've got going."

"Yeah, thirty and thirty-eight, it might raise some eyebrows, but I could handle it."

"Who says I'm looking for a man? You're definitely from the old school, Uncle Ray." Time to change the conversation. "By the way, when's your birthday?"

"Why do you ask that?"

"Because it's one of the ways you get to know people, asking for their birth date."

"September 15, if I recall right. I don't keep track much anymore. And yours?"

She delivered him a sly smile.

He sat straighter. "No, it's not today," he said, reading into her what he did not want to hear.

She smiled again, reveling in her teasing.

He, in turn, shook his head in disgust.

"Do you want me to go back to the cabin?" she asked.

"No, I want you to sit right there."

"Quietly."

"Yes, for now, until I catch up with your thinkin'."

The call she half expected came the following morning, while she was editing Mr. Stark's "sheets" from the oral history tapes.

"I'm not interrupting anything, am I?" Cory asked hesitantly.

"No, nothing important," she said, undecided as to the posture she would take to his calling.

"You know, things happened so fast the other day, Billie, I don't know whether either of us had time to think on them," he said in a conciliatory tone.

She'd been able to think of little else but. "That could be the case."

"I'd like very much for you to join me on another ride this weekend." He paused. "Maybe we could talk things over more, maybe find some middle ground where we could agree."

"If you mean on the meeting room question, I'm not sure there is much more to say." And on the other…she just didn't know.

"Some of our members were pretty upset. They're thinking I should go over your head and talk to the mayor or somebody."

"That's your choice." Her stomach knotted.

"I told them I wouldn't do it, that it was your decision. You planning on coming out for a ride this Saturday?"

She wanted to question him about the sleepy-eyed one, tell

him about what another member of his organization had been up to. Her sense from the conversation, however, was that he knew nothing of it. She decided to let it pass, rather than aggravate matters more.

"I have a full schedule this weekend, Cory. I'd like to take a rain check on your offer."

"Listen then, why don't we meet at the Buzzard's Roost Saloon this evening for a beer and bite to eat? The meeting room thing will be off the agenda. We'll just talk horses."

She had to admit; the guy could lead her into temptation as easily as he could lead a horse. "I have a full evening, Cory."

"Day is already booked full, huh?"

"Yes."

"Okay, fine." His tone became more abrupt. "You've got a rain check. Anyway, I just wanted to touch base with you and make sure there were no hard feelings."

"No hard feelings," she said, closing the conversation with the click of the receiver.

Was she, in fact, engaging in an act of discrimination? On what basis was she denying them access to the meeting room, other than on her own personal beliefs? And was she letting her personal disappointment in the man influence her professional position as the librarian?

The questions dogged her the remainder of the day. She attributed it to her inexperience, to her inability to draw on past practice. She was managing by instinct, a step below seat of the pants, an approach sure to place personal feelings above professional conduct. Was it her library or the public's? How would Mr. Whitington have answered the question?

"Have you ever been in the Buzzard's Roost Saloon?" she

asked her uncle during their after-dinner council.

"One time a fishing buddy of mine and I stopped in there for lunch a few years ago after an outing. I was out of uniform, however."

"Out of uniform? You mean they have a dress code?" She chuckled.

"No. It's just that I had my railroad cap on, while everyone one else in there wore baseball caps with farm logos."

"What's it like inside?"

He shrugged. "Like most every other roadside tavern, I expect. You have your usual bar–your jars of pickled eggs and sausages sitting on top of it, your sports trophies behind it, your dartboard, pool table, jukebox, dance floor, scattered tables and chairs. No booths, though, and that's about it. I think they have a band that comes in on weekends. I hear the place can get a little rowdy at times."

"Who owns the place?"

"Not sure. I think it's gone through several owners over the years."

"How's the food?"

"They have a big sign hanging in back of the bar that says 'best food for seventy-five miles.'" He glanced at her out of the corner of his eye. "What they don't say is there aren't many restaurants within seventy-five miles. But, the food's okay, unless you like to eat it off a plate."

"Oh?"

"Yeah, their menu is pretty much limited to sandwiches. They serve 'em in those plastic baskets with a pickle and chips. I had a shredded ham, if I recall right–not bad. Why are you asking? You plannin' on trying it out?"

"Cory called. He wanted to meet me there this evening."

She felt his gaze on her for a moment.

"Is that right? And I take it you said no, since you're sitting here."

"Yes. I don't think I would have felt comfortable, after all that's happened."

"I understand, but sometimes, you do have to be careful about lumpin' people together," he said, shifting in his lawn chair. "They all may belong to the same organization, but that don't mean they always share the same views, or the same intentions, or are aware at all times of what's going on with every member. Did I ever tell you the story of Fireball Franklin?"

"No, you haven't told me any story. Fireball Franklin, is he from around here?"

"He was from up around Jeff City way."

"Drat!" She leaned back with a laugh, glancing up at the clear, early evening sky. "For a second there, Uncle Ray, I was thinking you could be a candidate for my oral history class. I have to say, telling stories is as regular as eating around here. Okay, who was Fireball Franklin? I take it that wasn't his real first name."

He wagged his finger at her, silencing her teasing. "Fireball was a nickname. Raymond was his first name."

"Uh-oh."

"Yeah, another Ray. He was a pitcher for the Jeff City State Penitentiary baseball team back in the sixties and he was a great one. The guy had a fastball no one could hit."

"Who does a prison team play, other prison teams?"

"Yep as well as other semi-pro teams from around the state. One year he set an all-time Missouri state semi-pro record for strikeouts and led them into the state finals against a team from St. Joe. By that time he'd gotten a lot of notice in the press. With all those strikeouts he was racking up, he also had caught the eye of major league scouts."

"Why would they be interested in him, if he was locked away in prison?" she asked.

His eyes gleamed, warming to his story, obviously satisfied he'd caught her attention. "He had a parole hearing coming up right after the state final game. He was convinced all the hoopla would clinch his case for getting out. As for the big league teams, they felt his being an ex-convict could only add to his attraction.

"Anyway, they made it all the way to the state finals in St. Joe, where they were expectin' a record turnout of fans, mostly because of Fireball and his teammates. They added a new piece of excitement to the game. They were like a traveling zoo where you could go and watch the dangerous animals at play in your own backyard. Funny thing, the crowd was usually on their side. It had to do with the old American tradition of rootin' for the underdog. Most people saw them as the real underdogs, no question about it."

"Underdogs in life," she added, feeling the role of facilitator.

"Yeah. As it turns out, it was about a sixty-mile round trip to the ballpark where the championship game was to be played. As usual, they were being transported on a converted school bus."

"Were there guards on board?" she asked.

"Two guards, plus the driver." He paused, taking a sip of his tea. "In those days, they were stricter with the convicts, especially if there was to be any interaction with the public. They even kept 'em handcuffed during the ride."

"Excuse me for interrupting your story, Uncle Ray, but why would the prison allow them to take part in these games?"

"They saw it as a public relations move, a way of showin'

how they treated the prisoners and how they were preparin' them for a return to life on the outside by giving them a little taste of it. The problem was that Fireball considered himself the meal ticket for the team. He felt if it wasn't for him, his teammates wouldn't be enjoyin' those short jaunts into the free world. He also considered himself smarter than his teammates and therefore rarely spoke to them. The only guy he would speak to on a regular basis was his battery mate Bart Mosely."

"Battery mate is the catcher?"

"Right." He shook his head, no doubt pitying her poor baseball knowledge. "A pitcher needs to keep on good terms with his catcher. They're dependent on each other. Come the day of the final game, however, Mosely was sportin' a heavily bandaged right hand–said he tripped and landed on it during a workout. Fireball was befuddled by the guy's carelessness, but agreed with him in thinkin' whether he was in there or not wasn't going to make a helluva lot of difference."

"Did he have a replacement?" she asked.

"Yep, and a pretty good one, good enough not to screw things up. The thing that puzzled Fireball was Bart's nonchalant attitude toward missing the game. It wasn't at all like him. Normally, the game was never over for the guy. If he wasn't flashin' the pitcher signals or positioning the outfield, he was checkin' the team's bus schedule or packing equipment. Hell, he once spent an entire evening ironing uniforms by hand, when the prison laundry was forced to shut down the day before a game because of a power failure."

Uncle Ray adjusted himself in his chair and put his feet up, settling into his role as storyteller. He took a few swats at a pesky fly before resuming. "As the story goes, on the bus ride over to the championship game, Fireball began to humor Bart, knowing he'd be sitting this one out in the bullpen. 'Remember that game of stop-the-music we played over in Independence?' he asked him.

"The game he was referrin' to was one they were playin' before a crowd of pot-bellied boozers. Before the game even started, this organ grinder breaks into a medley of jailhouse tunes–*Folsom Prison Blues, I'm in the Jailhouse Now, Jailhouse Rock,* songs like that."

"Mood music," Billie quipped.

He shot her the silencing look again. "Well, they'd been targets of taunting fans in the past, but on this occasion, the barbs were really flyin' and were being relentlessly orchestrated by the organ guy. Fireball knew his catcher was overly touchy to fan reaction and sensed his rising anger as he tossed him his warm-up pitches.

"Suddenly, Bart rises from his squat position and marches toward the grandstand area. Fireball was ready to take off after him, when just as quickly he stops and again takes the squat position. Fireball then realized what his buddy was up to. Bart had stationed himself directly in line with the organist, but at an angle where the protective screen behind home plate no longer stood as a barrier between them and the grinder. Bart flashed the sign for a fastball and Fireball uncorked a trolley wire high over his receiver's head and straight toward the guy pounding away at the keyboard. All of a sudden, the guy looks up with this smile nailed on his face and sees this missile bearing down on him. It was so close he was lookin' cross-eyed at it. Well, he did manage to get his kisser out of the way in the nick of time, so the ball ended up bouncin' off a guardrail behind him. It sure pulled the plug on that music.

"'God, do you remember the look on the guy's face, when he came up for air?' Fireball reminded Bart, figuring his retellin' of the story would lift his spirits."

He paused for dramatic effect. "But it didn't."

"Had his heart set on playing in the championship game. Right, Uncle Ray?" Billie commented.

He lowered his head, peering over the rim of his tea glass at her. "Well, there was something else going on at the time which might have been a factor."

"What was that?"

"There was this young woman who began appearing at their games several weeks into the season. The players had noticed her always sitting alone in the far reaches of the bleachers. She was a classy lady and definitely a target for the players rovin' eyes. They agreed she was the sort of gal who belonged at a polo match or horse show."

"With her hair up in braids," she couldn't resist adding.

"Yeah, that kind. It wasn't long after that Bart told Fireball he'd begun to exchange messages with the lady. There was nothing surprising about that. The team had its share of groupies. They were celebrities, after all. But this gal was sure no groupie and why was she givin' all her attention to Bart? Fireball wondered. That was a little surprising. As much as Fireball liked the guy, the truth was, Bart was what a woman could expect on the other end of a blind date–a have-not."

"A mismatch," she added arbitrarily.

"Yeah, so much so Fireball was beginnin' to think there could be a conspiracy involved, a plot on the part of prison officials to expose any break attempts."

"A plant?" She nodded in understanding.

"A plant, though it just didn't figure. There was no mistakin' her attentions, however. Fireball noticed she held her applause only for Bart. The problem arose when she failed to show at their last game before the title contest. Fireball had noticed a break in Bart's concentration. It was something apparently still troublin' him on the ride over to this game. Then Bart really surprises him. He tells him she's big on poetry, reads it as a hobby. So, he had written one for her, and asks Fireball to take a look at it before he hits her with it, which flabbergasts Fireball. It was rare when he and Bart would stray from talkin' anything but baseball. Oh, they would bring up a few private matters, but only to skim them. One thing they did discuss was their reasons for being there in prison. For the same reason, it turned out."

"Which was?" Billie quickly interjected.

"Manslaughter. The details were never discussed, but Fireball guessed Bart's case to be like his. A few drinks, a fender bender, some hot words, and the next thing you know, some guy is threatening you with a tire iron and you got no choice but to level him with the car you happen to be driving at the time."

"So, what about the poem?" she said, her interest tweaked by the oddly sentimental angle in his testosterone driven tale.

"Fireball read it, told him it was nice, and said she'd like it, though he had no idea if she would. Bart then tells him he's already shown it to her. 'So, why you showin' it to me' he asks him. 'I wanted a second opinion,' he says, like he was askin' for a medical diagnosis. 'So, what was her reaction?' he asks. 'Her reaction was she didn't show up at the last game,' he answered.

"Fireball told him that for all they knew, she could've been sick. Either that or she was playing her own little game up in the stands, while they were playing theirs on the field. He told Bart he needed to get over it and that he was becoming too attached to life in the pen, too comfortable to doing time."

"Like professional students. They're unable to separate themselves from life in the student lounge," she said.

Uncle Ray nodded in agreement. "Well, Bart would have none of it. All he had to do was take a look at his uniform to remind himself of his contempt for the place. Somebody had come up with the great idea of putting pinstripes on the uniforms, except the pins were closer to being bars, thanks to some guy's sense of humor."

"It's called black humor."

"Whatever." Uncle Ray shrugged. "Bart was only playing along for the opportunity it provided him. He was prepared to take advantage of any break that came his way. He wasn't going to let anyone stand in his way, when the break came—"

"And this game was going to be his big break?" Billie leaned forward in anticipation.

"Yes, and there was a big turnout for it. According to the policy, the team entered the stadium by bus with each player still handcuffed. As they filed out, a guard would remove them. Other guards took up positions at various spots around the stadium to keep a watch on things.

"While Fireball was doin' his warm-up pitches with the back-up catcher, he scanned the stands several times to see if Bart's lady friend was in the crowd, but he couldn't spot her. It seemed strange not to have Bart taking his throws. He noticed him earlier in the bullpen; apparently resigned to his role as spectator and the fact his woman was a no-show. 'He'll just have to live with it,' Fireball thought."

Uncle Ray paused to give Buster a scratch on the ear and a pat on the head. "Well, ol' Fireball got off to a shaky start, walking several batters and pitching himself into several jams, before settling down. He soon was firing strikes again and the crowd was roarin' its approval. He was feelin' a fresh surge of enthusiasm, which got even better when the prison team pushed across a couple of runs to give them the lead. Ol' Fireball was back in the zone where he felt he could do no wrong. He saw himself as a man protecting his turf. The guy felt free as a bird on that mound and was determined to ride that feelin' all the way out of the slammer. All those guys on the outside who'd gone through all of the proper baseball upbringings–the little league, American Legion ball, baseball camps, they couldn't come close to matchin' ol' Fireball's determination. Fame was their motivatin' factor. Freedom was his. His only regret was Bart being unable to share in the moment.

"With a victory near, he strode to the end of the bench nearest the bullpen area to see if he could attract his teammate's attention, maybe give him a thumbs up to boost his spirits. From that distance, however, the figures were only a blur and difficult to make out. 'Have they left yet?' a teammate suddenly whispers in his ear, seeing Fireball staring toward the bullpen. 'What do you mean, *have they left yet?*' he asks the teammate. 'You know–have they left yet?' the teammate says again. Fireball glared past the dumb look on the guy's face to those of his other teammates sitting on the bench. Their wary eyes revealed something was up."

"Was he the only one who didn't know?"

"Apparently so. He looked again to the bullpen but didn't see any unusual activity, so he decided to take a closer look. Makin' like he was getting a drink, he jogged to a water fountain located along the restraining wall a short distance down the left field foul area. He bent to drink, knowing somewhere up in the stands a guard's eyes were trained upon him. He then rose from the fountain and again stared at the bullpen. Somethin' was screwy. Several players were climbing into the bus. Ahead of them looked to be their driver and a guard, the one assigned to watch the bullpen area. He knew it wasn't the normal boarding procedure he was watchin' and certainly not the time for it. 'They're goin' to go for it!' he thought to himself, 'just cruise on out of here in our bus. That's got to be it! It's so damn simple, no one will notice—'"

"They were hidden from view?"

"The area between the outfield fence and outer wall was not only where the bullpen was located but also where the bus was parked. The whole area was blocked from view. Only an access gate provided Fireball a peak and only then because he was positioned at a proper angle to see it. He decided right then and there they were going to pull it off. He was always good at sizing up game plans and knew that the simpler the plan, the fewer things to go wrong. It was merely a matter of execution.

"He reckoned they had only one choice and that was to travel the entire distance between the fence and outer wall, from left field to right where there was an employee exit gate. All the while they would be shielded from the view of the crowd and guards. He figured they already had seen to it that the exit gate was unlatched."

Buster picked up and moved from his master's feet to Billie's more attentive hand. Uncle Ray shot him a glance, clearly branding his dog a traitor, before continuing. "When the bus began to roll, ol' Fireball was like the drownin' man whose life is flashin' before him, except it was his future he was lookin' at and there was nothin' to see.

"A few paces to the left was a jeep used in dragging the field with a groundskeeper half-asleep slumped in the driver's seat. Fireball hijacked the thing, bullied the guy into giving him the keys, telling him the bullpen crew was making a break for it on their bus. He jumped into the jeep and headed directly across the diamond, the only path he could take, if he was to beat the bus."

"Wait!" she said. "You mean he was intending to drive right across the field? During the game?"

"That's right." Her uncle gave a tomahawk chop motion with his right hand, meaning straight across the diamond. "As he crossed the foul line into fair territory, and pounded the horn with his fist to warn the players on the field of his coming and the guards to his intention. He almost ran over the opposing team's shortstop who was camped under a pop fly as Fireball came rollin' through. A teammate let out a warning cry, which sent the guy scramblin' from Fireball's path. When he reached the right field area, he figured the bus must be equal distance from their destination. He could only imagine its presence behind the fence, but was confident he could win the race to the exit gate.

"The instant he re-entered foul territory, he hit the brakes. He was back on the gravel runway that circled the playing field, a couple of strides from the gate. Leaping from the jeep, he sprinted for the exit. By this time, fans were gatherin' round, fascinated at what was happenin'. Some were hop-scotchin' their way through empty seats to the scene of the commotion, and so were the security guards. 'Escape! Escape!' Fireball yelled.

"He checked the gate, and as he expected, it was unlatched, so he quickly snapped it to the closed position. He then turned in time to see the bus crawlin' toward the clearing from the path between the fences. It came to a complete stop not more than twenty-five feet from where he stood, close enough for him to recognize the figure behind the wheel. Bart had donned the driver's cap and jacket and was in command.

"That must have been a scene," Billie said, thoroughly

caught up in the story.

"You bet. It was a strange feelin' for Fireball, seeing his battery mate sitting there. He looked more at home in the driver's outfit than he did in a baseball uniform. He assumed Bart had seen him fiddling with the latch. And now that he'd planted himself directly in his path, figured he also understood his intention. He wished it were as easy to guess Bart's next move. The guy who with a wink of the eye, a nod of the head, or a flick of the wrist could give him a clue to his next move was sitting poker-faced, his hands grippin' the steering wheel, like he was waitin' for a light to change.

"Fireball thought the hell with this crap and took a step forward, but before he could take a second one, the bus came lungin' at him. He jumped from its path as the thing gathered momentum for an all-out effort to bust through the metal gate. Well, it bent but it didn't break. The sound of screechin' metal had hardly stopped before a swarm of guards and bystanders rushed in for a view of the massive hulk tangled in a net of steel. The guards carefully entered the opened doorway of the bus and escorted the prisoners out."

"Were there any injuries?" she asked.

Her uncle shook his head. "Except for some egos, no. Bart was the first to appear. As he walked down the steps, he paused to stare into the stands. He was jugglin' a ball in his hand. Fireball attempted to see what he was starin' at, thinkin' maybe he was still looking for his woman, but could see nothin' but patches of lingerin' fans waitin' for the final outcome. Bart finally turned his attention to Fireball who all of a sudden was overtaken by an awareness the two were no longer wearing the same uniforms.

"As a guard prepared to fix the handcuffs on him, Bart flashed Fireball a weak smile and tossed him the ball. Fireball caught it, studied it for a moment, and returned the smile. Ol' Fireball then wheeled and hurled the thing deep into the bleachers where it bounced around some empty seats, until some kid ran it down and carted it away.

"End of story," he said, jutting his hands out and squeezing his shoulders in a take-it-or-leave-it attitude.

As if on cue, Buster nudged her hand for more attention.

Billie caressed the dog's head absentmindedly as she contemplated Uncle Ray's story. "So, like Fireball, I shouldn't assume Cory to be an imitation of his cohorts," she said, following a lengthy pause. "Is that the message I'm to take from your story?"

"I'm not sayin' what message you should take. I only told a tale, like your oral history people do, though what you just said could be one of the little messages to come from it." He watched her, a wry grin splitting his benign face.

"One of the little messages?" She wrinkled her nose at him. "How about individual goals are often in conflict with organizational goals?"

He nodded slowly. "That sounds like it could be one."

"A little one?"

"Yeah, a little one."

"We often don't see ourselves as others see us?"

"Could be."

"Let's see—one little, two little, three little messages. Okay, I give up. What's the big one, Uncle Ray?"

"The message of this story?"

"Yes, what is it I'm to take from the story, if you don't mind saying?"

"The big message?"

"The biggie."

"Stay out of jail."

135

She crossed her arms, narrowed her eyes, and glowered at him.

"Yeah, I know. Now it's my turn to keep quiet," he said.

A self-imposed restriction he would have no trouble observing, she thought.

The sun dipped below the treetops, transforming the evening shades into an advancing dusk. A brisk southerly breeze, stirred by an approaching front, swept the hillsides, bringing with it the promise of rain.

She retrieved an old hairbrush and began to groom Buster's coat, keeping one eye on her uncle. She would wait for the head-nodding to start, so she could coax him into calling it a day.

The first nod came at exactly the same time the train whistle sounded, causing him to cock his head to the wind, like a bird to a beckoning mate, as the train made its pass. A second series of whistles, followed by a third, brought him abruptly to his feet to stare in the direction of the sounds.

She stopped her grooming, intrigued by her uncle's movements. "Something wrong, Uncle Ray?"

"Hear those whistles?" he asked, his tone clipped.

"Sure, I hear them," she replied, curious as to why he would ask.

"Listen to the pattern." He jerked his head in the direction of the train. "Hear that? A long blast followed by three short ones. The pattern is usually two long blasts, followed by a short one and another long one, meaning they're approaching a crossing and people should be on the lookout for them."

"So, what does three short ones and a long one mean?" She resumed her brushing of the dog.

"It means fire."

"Fire?" Billie's hand froze in mid-air.

"Train crews are trained to keep their eyes peeled for fires. If they spot one, they're instructed to sound the alert. That's what the engineer is doin'. I'm going to get my binoculars."

Uncle Ray strode quickly towards the door. "While I'm doing that, why don't you go grab the ladder from my tool shed?"

She had the ladder upright and against her uncle's house by the time he returned with the binoculars.

"Here," he said, handing them to her. "You take a look. Unfortunately, my eyes have grown old along with the rest of me."

She climbed the ladder, crawled onto the roof, and peered through the lenses, spotting nothing but deepening darkness.

"I'm not seeing anything," she called to her uncle.

Suddenly, sirens could be heard in the distance, replacing the train whistles in their frequency and intensity.

She scanned the skyline again, attempting to make out shapes and sizes. Were those billows of smoke or cloud formations that were adding an eerie orange cast to the moon?

Tension entered her like a contagion, as sirens wailed in the night.

Her uncle yelled from below, "I'm going to go call—"

"Wait–wait," she snapped. "*Oh, God.*"

Amid the murk, a bright plume of flame shot skyward, as if someone had just flicked their lighter on in the distance, the red tongue oscillating for a moment, before bending to the wind–toward them. An instant later, a second tongue appeared, and then a third.

The sirens grew closer. A vehicle mounted with a public address system could be heard ordering an immediate evacuation.

"We'd better get out," she called down to her uncle.

"I'll start hosing the place down," he called back.

"No, Uncle Ray," she yelled, her voice rising with anxiety. "We won't have the time. Besides, a hose isn't going to do any good with this."

They hurriedly backed their trucks into position and scrambled to load their personal belongings. She gauged the fire to be about ten miles away. Considering the wind speed, they should have a half-hour to grab and run...at the most.

Sheriff and Fire Department officials were rushing door to door, ordering residents to leave.

"Which way is the evacuation route?" she called to one of them.

"Take the highway east out of town. The road headed west is barricaded," he yelled back.

The scent of smoke, borne by the steady wind, descended on the town. In the distance, an enormous halo of light rimmed the horizon. The fear became palpable the moment the first blowing embers and firebrands from the advancing flames rained down on them.

"You've got to get out now, folks!" a fire official warned them on his final pass. "The fire already has entered the edge of town."

She loaded her last items, fighting back the urge to go back for more. Her uncle was in the cab of his truck, Buster alongside, waiting for her.

"Go ahead, Uncle Ray. I'll be right behind you."

The moment he took off, she hopped into her truck to follow. Slowly, she edged the vehicle forward, eyeing her uncle's movements, as he made his way onto a side street leading to the highway where a couple of other lagging cars fell in between him.

Confident of his escape, she swung her truck sharply

around and headed down the dirt path leading to the library. The instant she entered the roadway she had to swerve to avoid a fire official's car coming in the opposite direction. She eyeballed the rearview mirror, as the guy slammed his car to a stop, jumped from the driver's seat, and in the glow of his rotating beacons, flailed his arms in anger, or warning, or both at her.

Billie raced the truck down the path, through a swirl of embers that already had ignited a score of rooftops. She knew it was only a precursor of what was to come. Flames were licking from treetops, waiting impatiently for the next gust of wind to propel them forward.

She flipped on the truck's air conditioner as the intensifying heat outside infiltrated her cab. To her right ran a landscape of burning homes and trees, to her left, like a loyal companion, the Jacks Fork.

Her means of escape…if necessary.

As she neared the library, she could see thick columns of smoke rising from the center of town. The fire line was no more than a block or two from the river.

"No! No!" she shouted, pounding the steering wheel, on seeing ringlets of fire eating away at the library's roof.

She pulled to a stop at the foot of the porch and braced herself for what awaited outside. Hurling open the door, she instantly was knocked to her knees by the combination of wind, smoke, and heat. Righting herself, she snatched a towel from the cab, fumbled for her keys, and sprinted for the entrance. The instant the lock broke free, she burst through the door and up the stairwell to the meeting room. Seizing a folding chair, she scampered to the reading room and the corner bookcase.

Gripping the chair by its legs, she swung it against the glass panels with all the force she could muster, shattering them into shards. She reached in to retrieve the books, wrapping them in the towel. In the same instant, a brilliant light illuminated the room. The wind fanned the flames, pre-cooking the building for the firestorm's final assault.

She bounded back down the stairs and out the door, only to be met again by a blast of smoke-filled air. Choking on the fumes, she struggled to her truck.

"*Owww*! Dammit!" she cried, letting go of the red-hot door handle. She took a portion of the towel to shield her hand and yanked it open, then jumped into the cab and ignited the engine. It took a couple of cranks to start it up, but it was still alive.

Ash covered her front window, so she switched on the wipers to clear it. At the same time a nauseous odor set off an inner alarm. An ember had lighted on her hair, setting it afire. She flailed wildly at the flame, extinguishing it with her towel, but not before it singed the back of her neck.

Swinging the truck around, she was stunned to see the road she came in on engulfed in flames. The wildfire had reached the river.

She was left with no choice. Unable to bear the smoke and heat any longer, and feeling faint, she aimed the truck directly at the river and slammed her foot on the accelerator. Wheels churning, embers flying, she steered it over a narrow embankment and through a stretch of shallow water and onto a gravel bar where she parked it. She then plucked from the floor of the passenger side a small cooler, removed the books from the towel, and sealed them inside the container. Quickly slipping the belt from her jeans, she looped it around the cooler's handle, creating a shoulder strap for her to carry it.

She was not about to let go of the family jewels.

Clutching the towel, Billie jumped from the vehicle and

ran directly downstream, sloshing and stumbling through ankle-high–waist-high–chest-high water, before hurling her body into the river's arms. She disappeared below the surface, maneuvering herself into a crouching position, letting the balm of the cool waters soothe her weary mind and body, until the need for air drove her back up.

The moment she surfaced, gasping for breath, she took the drenched towel and threw it over her head. From beneath it she could glimpse the inferno as it neared its zenith. With each gust of wind, tongues of fire leapt from treetops to lick at limbs dangling seductively from the opposite bank. Occasionally, the two would connect, creating an arc of flame and a shower of ash and ember, each burning fragment emitting an audible hiss upon hitting the water.

She transferred her makeshift shoulder strap to her wrist, allowing the cooler to float on the surface as she made her descents, which were becoming ever more frequent. Aware she was losing the battle for precious air with the oxygen-devouring firestorm, she drifted into a delirium. Images of her parents floated in and out of her near subconscious state.

In a moment of resignation, she decided to unhook the strap and set the cooler free. Surely, a searcher would locate it and her uncle or a colleague would divine her intent, just as she accounted for her parents' final act.

She rose to the surface and was struggling to loosen the strap, when she heard a sharp cracking sound from above. At first she thought it might be the last clack of a disintegrating tree, but then realized it was something heaven sent. *The cold front was passing through.*

Billie looked toward the sky, through the choking smoke and flying debris, and felt the first drop of rain buss her cheek. A second clap of thunder loosened the firmament, transforming the drops into a deluge.

She screamed her delight, yanking the towel from around her head. The inferno still raged, but now it had another force of nature to contend with.

Steadily, over what seemed like hours, the firestorm was drained of its intensity. Flames, stretching a hundred feet high, shrank like lighted wicks reduced to normalcy by an invisible hand.

The torrent continued late into the night, further diminishing the fire.

At last, Billie stood and walked to shallow water, her entire body shriveled like a raisin. Nauseated by the lingering fumes, she retched. Attempting a deep breath, she retched again, coughing with dry heaves and fatigue. Gathering herself, she shuffled to an embankment and collapsed, cooler in hand.

Some time later, she awoke with a start to an otherworldly scene. The rain had stopped. What time was it? Was that a smoky pall hanging in the air or an early morning fog?

Moments later, a shaft of sunlight broke through the murk, followed by another. The dawn of a new day.

All around her she could see curls of smoke rising from blackened tree stumps and remnants of fire flickering here and there. Her truck still stood on the gravel bar, its tires deflated, and its paint blistered by the searing heat.

Mr. Whitington's library and card catalog were no more, reduced to smoldering rubble like every other structure in sight.

Looking out over the devastation, she began to weep. In only a short time she'd made this her home, yet it had seemed so long. And now it too was gone. Like her parents.

Perhaps it would have been better if the rains had not come, she pondered in a moment of despair.

On the brink of dozing off once more from fatigue, she caught a movement from across the river, one that brought a beam to her eyes. Silhouetted against the gray landscape, a female deer, stepping cautiously, approached the water's edge. Entranced, she watched the doe thrice touch her mouth to the water.

She'd finally seen her deer.

"Billie! Billie. *Billie*."

The sounding of her name sent the doe scampering from the water. It was her uncle calling from somewhere along the dirt road. Climbing to her feet, reeking of smoke and chilled to the bone, she went to greet him.

Buster was the first to reach her, backing her up with his joyful leaps. Her uncle followed with a warm embrace.

"Careful, you're going to get wet," she advised him.

"Where in the hell have you been, young lady?" he asked, gripping her by the shoulders, his eyes suspiciously wet. "You had me scared to death."

"Celebrating my birthday," she murmured weakly.

"What the—"

He'd spotted her truck stranded on the gravel bar.

"Did you ride out this firestorm in the river?"

She nodded.

He hugged her close, oblivious to her wet condition. "Are you okay?"

"I got singed in a couple of places," she said, sniffing back tears.

He held her back from him, looking over her shoulder. "Jesus, is that stuff smolderin' in the back of your truck your belongings?"

She nodded again. "Where is everyone? Did they all get out safely?"

"They all got out in time. Now they all want to get back in, but the fire officials won't let them until the place is declared safe. Buster and I managed to slip through the barricades unnoticed."

"Our homes?"

"Up in smoke like everything else."

"Oh, Uncle Ray." For once, words failed her.

He patted her back. "Don't worry, the place was insured. Come on, let's go."

"Go where?" The enormity of the situation was still too much for her to grasp.

"To my truck. It's parked out on the highway. We need to get you checked out."

"What about my truck? Maybe we can get it started."

"I doubt if there is any start left in it. Besides, it isn't goin' far on those tires. We'll worry about it later."

"Just a moment," she said. "I need to get something."

She walked wearily down to the bank, returning with her cooler strapped to her shoulder. And to a place and future, neither of which existed at the moment.

Chapter Nine

A slow-moving column of incoming emergency crews and National Guard troops met them on the way back, just as they had completed a walk-by inspection of the charred remains of their homes. One of the vehicles stopped to give them a lift to her uncle's truck.

From there they traveled to a Red Cross evacuation center located outside of Van Buren where Billie received a complete medical check-up along with some ill-fitting dry clothes. She'd suffered small first-degree burns on the back of her neck and upper left arm from the embers. Though painful, she was advised they would heal on their own without scarring within two to five days.

She was fortunate, the doctor said, for she'd already received, in effect, the basic emergency treatment—which was to run cold water over the burns as soon as possible, and, better yet, to put cool, water-soaked cloths over them.

The rushing, cold waters of the Jacks Fork, it appeared, had healed her naturally.

The emergency center bustled with activity, as displaced families, relief officials, grief counselors, and media representatives from across the country mingled in an atmosphere of shock, sorrowful reunion, and confusion. Though no visible signs of injury to those gathered around her were apparent, Billie recognized the likelihood of a serious emotional toll. Perhaps, the shock itself was serving as an insulator, numbing the victims, including herself, to the reality

145

that had befallen them.

Following her parents' death, she'd read there was no standard pattern of reaction to a calamitous event. Some individuals react immediately, while others exhibit delayed responses. Experts agreed that in the normal course of events, individuals who had handled previous traumatic events in their lives were more likely to cope successfully.

So she should be just fine, shouldn't she?

The immediate issue facing them was shelter, finding a safe haven where they could relax and converse with friends and family in privacy. Some chose to stay with relatives, while others had the option of taking up temporary residence in furnished on-campus apartments at nearby Ozarks State College where classes had broken for the summer, or in base housing at Fort Leonard Wood, a further distance away. A fourth alternative was to rent a motel room, an expensive proposition, considering the length of stay that might be required.

In the end, after consulting with each other and friends, Billie and her uncle signed up for the apartments, Uncle Ray arguing he'd already been in the army but not to college. It turned out to be a popular choice. A number of other Woodland Hills residents, wishing to stick together, took the same option, including Shirley, Scott, and their families. Connecting with friends would give them an opportunity to share their experiences and vent the stress bit by bit.

So, they started over. They purchased some basic essentials in Van Buren, loaded them onto her uncle's truck, and made their way to the school complex where they took adjoining apartments on the first level, down the hall from her co-workers. Scott alone was excited to a degree, claiming he had been considering attending the school, anyway, and this would give him the opportunity to scope it out.

It was a relatively new college whose buildings, from the residence halls to the classroom structures, shared similar block designs and earth-tone exteriors–almost a pre-fabricated look, Billie decided. Yet, the apartments were clean and they were thankful, not to mention grateful for being alive and together.

Once settled, her first order of business was to check the cooler. Positioning it on a stand next to a window, she first wiped its surface clean with a damp cloth, then drew a deep breath and unsealed the top. Removing the books, she perused the pages carefully for evidence of water damage. She detected none. Next she sniffed their covers for lingering odors and once more found them free of impairment. Satisfied with their condition, she placed them back in the container and the container into a closet.

Later in the day, a county official dropped by to notify them of a "What happened–What next?" town-hall-type meeting to be held the next morning at the evacuation center. A good idea, she believed, skimming the flyer he left behind, particularly the part about jobs.

One thing she knew for sure, she wouldn't have to be making any decisions about computers. That one had been taken off her agenda. In fact, she had no agenda. The truth was she had been living a life of start-and-stop stories. The parent thing, the computer thing, the Cory thing–they all had beginnings, inadequate middles, and no ends.

Geared for a good night's rest, she stayed up only long enough to catch the national evening news, which led with the Woodland Hills story. Film footage was comprised mainly of aerial shots and interviews with survivors and fire officials, the firestorm having spent its fury long before the arrival of camera crews. The commentator closed with a mention of an ongoing investigation as to the cause of the conflagration.

"Can you hear me back there?" a barrel-chested man with a cherub face asked, shoving the microphone nearly into his mouth, and then giving it a couple of taps to boot. The sound reverberated throughout the auditorium.

Yes, Billie could hear him.

"For those of you who don't know me, I'm Dan Booker, sheriff of these parts. I know this has been a very difficult experience for you. However, we wanted to take this opportunity to bring you up to date on exactly what happened and what you should expect down the road. Before we get started, let me give a big thanks to all the emergency people, from the federal on down to the local levels, for their heroic efforts in dealing with this disaster."

He paused, a solemn look drawing out his face, until the applause died down. "Let me also give a big thanks to you citizens for your cooperation in the evacuation."

If ever a crowd yearned for answers, this one did, Billie thought, glancing around at the sea of concerned faces.

"It went remarkably well, considering you had little advance warning. Amazingly, there were no deaths or serious injuries associated with the event and for that, I think we can all be grateful," he said to another round of applause. "Now, the first thing I'm going to do is introduce you to Mark Finley. He's the district supervisor for the U.S. Forest Service and will summarize for you the course of the fire. I say the course of the fire, because he will not be addressing the cause of the fire. I'll do that when he finishes. Mr. Finley?"

A wiry man with frizzled, copper-colored hair, in formal Forest Service uniform, stepped briskly to the podium. "As the sheriff mentioned, I will brief you on the course of the fire and attempt to give you an idea of what happened. If I could have the lights dimmed, please."

Someone flipped a switch and on a large screen mounted aside the podium a photo appeared.

"This is an aerial shot taken yesterday afternoon showing the burn area. Down at the bottom of the screen, where you see these darkened areas, is where the fire began. It covers about a two-mile area and parallels the loop of the railroad tracks running south of Woodland Hills. Given the conditions–a stiff wind, dry underbrush, and timber, the fire quickly took hold. It is what we sometimes refer to as a passive crown fire as opposed to an active one."

"What do you mean by that?" an elderly man shouted.

"Okay, here's what I mean." He took a yard stick and pointed to the photo on the screen. "Crown fires start in the underbrush and crawl quickly to the treetops, or the crowns of the trees. Once they reach that point and with the aid of a strong wind they then travel treetop to treetop at great speed. The difference between an active and a passive crown fire is that an active requires a steep slope to travel up. If it has one, it can move up to thirty miles per hour and shoot flames 200 feet high."

No need to convince her how high, Billie thought, recalling the pillars of fire that had hovered over her.

"In this particular case, though the wind was brisk, it was not a gale-force one. Combine that with the fact that the incline in this immediate region is not as severe as others and you have, like I said, a passive crown fire. Now, let me be clear about this. A passive crown fire can cause as much damage as an active one. It just moves relatively slower. I say relatively because it moves much faster than the many brush fires we're used to in this area. All you need to see are some carcasses of dead rabbits and squirrels to determine that. So much for the myth that fires in Missouri move slower."

The crowd responded with a weak smattering of laughter.

"Okay, notice that the origin of the burn was fairly broad-based, almost exactly to the width of Woodland Hills. The sheriff will be touching on this point in a minute. The fire caused widespread damage on its initial run, and as you can see here, it overran Woodland Hills in full force. Not until it reached the Jacks Fork did it begin to break up. You'll also note the narrower swathes of burns at those points where it jumped the river." He carefully followed his comments with the pointer. "But for the rainstorm, it might have run a ways further, though with the daylight hours, I'm confident the fire crews could have contained it. Unfortunately, it popped up at the wrong time and wrong place for Woodland Hills. If someone could flip the lights back on, I'm going to turn this back over to Sheriff Booker."

Returning to the podium, the sheriff accidentally clipped the mike, sending out a sharp squeal that momentarily broke the audience's concentration.

"Okay, you heard Mr. Finley mention where the fire started, which was along the railroad tracks. Here's what we have thus far uncovered in our investigation, and this is also for the benefit of any media who are present."

He cleared his throat and shuffled some papers on the podium. "As the train started to make its southern loop below Woodland Hills, it slowed almost to a crawl, due to the sharp bend in the tracks. Shortly after the train began its turn, somebody took a long piece of rope that had been doused with gasoline, tied it to the undercarriage of one of the cars, and lit it. For the next several miles, the burning rope dangled along the tracks, igniting one accumulation of dry underbrush after another. It was not until the freight had nearly completed its loop that the crew discovered what was happening. That was the origin of the fire. As of now we have no suspects."

"It was those militia guys, Dan, and you know it!" a man barked from the audience.

The sheriff quickly raised his hands with palms out in a self-defense motion. "No, I don't know it. All I can say at the moment is we're not ruling anyone or anything out. The investigation is ongoing."

"What possible motive could anyone have to do something like this?" asked an older woman, unable or unwilling to disguise the anguish in her voice.

"There's a bag full of motives for people to commit arson, ma'am—a compulsion of some kind, fraud, vandalism, revenge, sabotage. Determining a motive is one of the major focuses of our investigation."

"What about water drops, why weren't there any of those," shouted someone from the back.

"I'll let Mr. Finley answer that," the sheriff said, motioning to the Forest Service representative, who stepped back to the mike.

"Water drops are usually done over on the West Coast where the fires can range up to 50,000 acres," he explained. "A fire has to exceed 1,000 acres to be considered a major fire, which this one did, of course." He paused, as if carefully considering his response. "We don't have many of them. Most of our fires can be put out in a day. Having water-drop capability is an expensive proposition. This fire, though a large one, was too short-lived to have been fought effectively from the air, anyway."

Holding a hand up to stave off another round of questions, the sheriff leaned forward. "I tell you what," he continued, "to answer any further questions you might have, and I'm sure there are many, we have set up tables around the room for you to meet with government and private sector officials. They should be able to answer your questions, including any you might have regarding housing, financial assistance, food assistance, and job status for those of you who are understandably concerned about your employment situation. The tables are clearly marked, so please, take the opportunity to talk to the representatives."

It may have been too soon for her to form an opinion, but from all outward appearances, her uncle seemed right in his judgment of the sheriff. There was a sincerity and sense of determination in his manner that bespoke a man of competence and conviction.

Billie was attempting to track down the mayor amid the general commotion following the briefing, when she heard a woman's voice call out her name.

"Miss Staley? Miss Staley?"

"Yes," she said, quickly identifying the woman as a media rep from her professional dress and detached demeanor.

"I'm Jennifer Parker from WXZT-TV in St. Louis. Can I ask you a couple of questions?"

"About what?"

"I understand it was your truck authorities found stranded in the middle of the river. Is that correct?" she asked politely, at the same time waving to attract her cameraman's attention.

"That's correct." Billie answered slowly, reluctantly. She'd faced the local media after her parents' plane crash, having to relive her nightmare in front of strangers. She had no wish to repeat the experience.

"Can you tell us how it got there?"

"I put it there."

"During the fire?"

"Yes," she answered reluctantly.

"Listen, my cameraman is standing right over there. I'd like to get this on film, if it's okay with you." She waved more frantically to him.

Billie inched away, searching for an escape. "I would prefer not."

"I think it would make a very interesting segment—why and how you came to spend the entire night in the river riding out the firestorm. I'm sure the public would find it a fascinating story."

"But it's my story and one I'd like to keep private."

The reporter stepped closer to her, pressing in, thrusting the microphone in her face. "Then it's true?"

"I didn't say that. Now, if you'll excuse me, I need to locate someone." She slipped back into the bustle, and continued her search for the mayor.

She had to admit he seemed humbled by the whole experience, though it didn't prevent him from giving her a longer-than-necessary hug, which she stoically endured. As for a prognosis for the town and specifically for her job, he had none. He was a mayor without a town and she was a librarian without a library. That's where matters stood. There was no precedent to go by, they agreed.

"Look, we still have a paycheck coming in," he said. "I'm just not sure for how long. We'll be sitting down with state officials to weigh the options. Meanwhile, I wouldn't blame you if you started to look elsewhere for employment opportunities, since there are no guarantees as to what will happen here."

"We don't even have a place to pick up our checks." She grimaced.

"Turn in your temporary address at the table marked 'City Government.'" He patted her shoulder. "We'll make sure it gets sent to you."

She hesitated, making sure she had her priorities in order before proceeding. "I'd better call the state library and let them know what the situation is."

"Good idea. And while you're at it, tell them they no longer need to be leaning on us for that computer decision. Christ, you can't say there's no good to come from this crisis."

"So what happens to Mr. Whitington's estate?"

"I haven't had time to think about it." He sighed, rubbing the back of his neck. "I seem to recall there was some wording spelling out how the funds would be re-channeled in case his directives were not complied with. I guess that would apply in this situation–but who knows? The lawyers will have to figure it all out."

The mayor, rocking back on his heels, continued with his directions to her. "Meanwhile, Billie, I'll give to you the same advice I've been giving others. Sit down with your family, your uncle–how's he doin' by the way?"

"Fine, he's around here someplace." She glanced around for him, not having seen him in the last little while.

"Sit down with him, take stock of your situation, and decide what the best course of action is for you, okay?"

"Okay," she said, somewhat taken aback by the efficacy of what he had to say.

They tried to sort it all out over lunch in her apartment.

"What a mess, Uncle Ray," she said between bites of her sandwich.

"Yep. They don't come much bigger than this."

"Where's Buster?" She was actually missing the old

hound.

Her uncle thumbed his finger over his shoulder. "Next door."

"Why didn't you bring him over?"

"Knocks over things."

"I don't care if he knocks over everything."

"Yes you do and don't get testy." He wagged his finger at her. "This isn't the time for it."

"You must think I'm a witch," she said, not hiding the disgust in her voice.

From the way his jaw dropped, she must have really surprised him.

"A witch? What makes you say that?"

"I say it because here you are living a nice, tranquil life in the country, hardly a worry in the world, and along comes your niece and presto, your home and hometown are gone. I came here to land on my feet and ended up landing on you."

"It's not your fault, and don't forget, Woodland Hills had also become your hometown."

She watched him anxiously, almost incredulously. "Don't you want to get just a little bit angry?"

He shrugged. "Not over things I can't control and that definitely includes you."

"You do know you have a right to be angry?"

"At who?"

"At whoever did it. They destroyed your property, for God's sake!"

"Then it wasn't a witch?"

"*Nooo,*" she said, dropping the remainder of her sandwich in feigned frustration. "What are we going to do, Uncle Ray?"

He squeezed her hand where it rested on the table. "We take it one step at a time by doin' the practical things, instead of sitting around fretting. The first thing I'm going to do is check on my property insurance. I suggest you do the same with your truck."

"Can I borrow yours tomorrow?"

"My truck? Sure. To check on yours?"

"Yes and to stop by the sheriff's office."

"For what?"

"There's a question I want to ask him," she said, rising from the table.

"Tell me, what could be drivin' you to go to the sheriff's office?" His curious gaze followed her.

"Anger," she said, pausing to give him a peck on the cheek.

Billie decided to drive the short distance to Plainville and take a chance on his being in rather than calling ahead for an appointment, which could mean a week or more delay. It had been her experience that government officials, even busy ones, more often than not would find the time to meet a walk-in constituent, especially one dangling a message not easily dismissed.

"Yes, my name is Billie Staley. I was wondering if Sheriff Booker is in. I'd like to see him, if possible," she said to the woman at the receiving desk.

"May I tell him what this is about?" she asked, revealing his presence.

"It concerns the investigation into the firestorm."

The receptionist dialed an extension and relayed the message in a bland monotone, pausing to listen to the reply, offering no hint as to the verdict.

"The sheriff will see you, Miss Staley. Just step on in to his office." She pointed across the hall.

"Miss Staley, you're Ray Staley's niece, I presume," he said, rising in greeting.

He appeared the professional, in keeping with her uncle's judgment of him.

"Thank you for seeing me." She shook his hand. "I know you're busy, sheriff, and I appreciate your giving me this time."

He resumed his seat behind his desk, motioning her to a chair across it. "So, you have something concerning the investigation. I'd have thought it might have had something to do with the guy who was bothering you, but he's still locked up."

"No, it's not about him."

"Then what's on your mind?"

"You mentioned at your briefing that the arsonist—"

"It could be arsonists."

"Or arsonists–used a rope to ignite the fire."

"That's correct."

"Is the rope still available?"

"The portion that didn't burn is." He steepled his fingers, watching her intently. "Why?"

"There's a chance I may know where it came from."

"Oh, is that right?" He arched a brow.

"Yes, unless you already have made a determination."

"No, we haven't, though we've done some checking."

"May I see it?"

"You think you could recognize a piece of rope?"

"This one I could. It is not the kind you see every day."

"How so," he asked, leaning forward in his chair.

She clearly had tweaked his interest. "It is exceptionally large in width and length, somewhat frayed, and made exclusively of natural fibers."

"How big in circumference, would you say?"

"Around two inches." She demonstrated with her fingers.

"How many braids?"

"Three, if I recall correctly."

He smiled. "Our investigators said pretty much the same thing. It's made from Manila hemp, one of the stronger natural fibers. Not the kind of rope you'd find on the market today. We checked some regional stores anyway and found no record of one that size being purchased recently," he said, rising again. "The evidence room is down the hallway. Let's take a look."

She followed him down a corridor to a half-door with a counter on top where a uniformed deputy received them. They signed a form attached to a clipboard and stepped through the door into a large room.

Directly across from the entrance was a line of olive drab lockers. To their left stood a block of cubicles stuffed with cell phones, computers, clothing, car stereo sets, guns, and assorted other items. To their right were piles of boxes and plastic bags marked "*burglary*," "*arson*," and "*homicide.*"

"What's in the lockers?" she asked the sheriff.

"Bags of dope, mostly."

"How long is this stuff kept here?"

"Depends. For lost and found property, it's usually ninety days. For most other items, it's at least ninety days following a conviction, unless it's evidence used in a murder, then it can be stored indefinitely, since appeals can drag on for years."

He walked to a corner where a large, clear plastic bag labeled "*arson*" was placed. He picked it up and held it to the light. "Can you see it?"

"Yes, I can," she said, studying the content.

"Well?"

"That's our rope." She sighed.

"Your rope?"

"The library's."

"Let's go back to my office," he said, replacing the bag.

Once settled back into their chairs, the sheriff reached for a pad of paper and a pen. "Okay, tell me about the rope."

Billie could see that his interest was tweaked. "It was part of a collection of collectibles dating back to the old mill, which were stored in our basement. We decided to set up a public display of them, including the rope, on the library's porch. The rope was later stolen."

"By whom?"

She shrugged. "We don't know."

"When?"

"I was notified of it Monday."

"By who?"

"By a volunteer. She was alerted to it by a patron who had noticed it missing."

He focused on his notes as he continued his questions. "So, it could have happened over the weekend or on Monday."

"Yes."

"Miss Staley, one of the reasons I'm glad you came in is that I've had it on my schedule to talk to you, anyway." He did look at her now, leaning back in his seat. "We've been checking into some of the local militia group's activities and one of the items brought to my attention is a meeting they had at the library, the one I believe the mayor had alerted me to. This is the same group, right?"

"Right."

"And they met at the library on Monday, is that right?"

"Yes, Monday morning."

"You don't by chance know what was discussed at the meeting, do you?"

"No."

"Has it crossed you mind that one of the militia guys could have lifted the rope?"

"It has, since you mentioned a rope being used in the arson."

He paused in his note-taking. "Do you personally feel they did?"

"I don't know sheriff. It's a possibility."

"One thing I intended to talk to you about concerns their leader, a guy by the name of Cory Winslow, one of the few who admits to being a member." He now watched her intently. "Do you know him?"

"Yes." Her stomach knotted. "He came to talk to me after the meeting about future use of the room by his group. He wanted to book it for the next month."

"Did you let him?"

"No. It was already was booked for the date he wanted."

"During the course of our investigation, it was brought to my attention that you were a friend of Mr. Winslow. Is that correct?

Somewhere in the back of her mind she knew this would surface. Now, she could only steel herself for the consequences.

"Who said that?" She gripped the arms of her chair.

"Someone who'd heard him mention it."

"A militia guy?" she asked, hoping it wasn't one of her staff.

"Yes."

"I would say more of an acquaintance. I've been on rides at his stable on two occasions. It's where I came to know him."

"There's no connection between you knowing him and his use of the meeting room then?"

"I didn't know he was a member of the militia, much less

its president, until he came into my office to sign the application. I don't mind telling you I was shocked." She forced her mind away from the painful memory to the more painful present. "Why do you ask? Do you think there's a connection?"

"I don't think you would have been questioning their use of the meeting room beforehand, if there was."

"Yes, but it was the mayor who decided to defer to you on it. You don't think I'm involved with the militia in some way, do you?"

"No, I don't, but I need to cover all the bases." He glanced back to his notes.

"The idea they may have planned this in the library makes my skin crawl. I should have sat in on their meeting, then maybe all of this could have been prevented."

"I've learned in this business, Miss Staley, that second guessing only leads to more second guessing and little else. Here's what you can do and it's something I may have to do myself down the road. Talk to your staff, pick at their memories regarding the stolen rope. Maybe somebody will recall something."

"I'll do that," she said absentmindedly.

"What's wrong?"

"I still feel this uncertainty hanging in the air about my being involved somehow, and I have nothing to disprove it."

"You already have something," he said matter-of-factly.

"The mayor's phone call? That's a little weak. It could even be considered a subterfuge to legitimize the meeting."

"No, it's not the mayor's phone call. It's that truck of yours parked in the middle of the river, and how we learned it got there, a story related to me by your uncle after the evacuation center briefing." He grinned, the first lightening of his expression she'd seen. "One doesn't go barreling into the middle of a fire if they were somehow involved in setting it. They may watch it from a distance, but not put themselves in the middle of it."

"Believe me, it's an experience I will never forget."

"By the way, that's another thing you can do." He peered at her from lowered brows. "Get the truck towed, unless you plan on becoming an urban legend of some kind."

"No, I intend to do it as soon as I leave here." She stood, greatly relieved. "And thank you, sheriff."

Billie decided on a pizza party for three–she, Shirley, and Scott–for her staff sit-down. The thick aroma of the pepperoni pizza, along with the pattering of a light rain on the roof of the porch, created a cozy atmosphere.

"Mr. Stark cornered me after the briefing," Shirley said, catching up a bit of dangling cheese. "He was looking for you."

"For what?"

"Hoped you were still planning on hearing his story. Can you believe it? The man's house was destroyed and all he was worried about was telling his story."

Billie shook her head. "It must be a dilly."

"He said it had something to do with a brawl between two midgets and a drunken minister."

"Mr. Stark sure knows how to put the oral into an oral history program." Billie chuckled.

Shirley grinned. "By the way, did you know he once was an owner of the Buzzard's Roost Saloon?"

"Why does that not surprise me? How long did he have it?"

"About five years, he said. He gave it up, when his wife

found religion. He had her working there as a waitress, so she could keep tabs on the help and make sure they weren't ripping him off. Apparently, the religion thing didn't work out for them. They ended up divorcing."

"Sounds like you got a preview of his story." Billie reached for another slice.

Shirley winked. "Yes, but he's saving the best for you."

"Has anyone been back in town to take a look at the fire damage?"

"I have," muttered Scott, his mouth full of pepperoni.

"What's it like?" Shirley asked, giving him no time to swallow.

"A moonscape is what it reminded me of. There's nothing left standing. Ash all over the place."

"Did you see the library?" Billie asked.

"Didn't see it. Saw the ground it was on."

"What did it look like?"

"A pile of rubble."

Her heart sank. Yet she'd known that would be the case. "I called the state library this afternoon to touch base with them on the situation," she said. "They offered to send in a bookmobile as a temporary measure, if you can believe that. I told them it would be fine, if it had only been the library that burned down. Can you picture a lone bookmobile sitting out there?"

"It's the thought that counts," Shirley said. "Do you think they will rebuild?"

"Will the city rebuild? Is that what you're asking?"

"Yes."

"I don't know the answer to that. If they do, it won't be anytime soon. Do you plan on rebuilding?"

"To be honest, we were thinking of selling anyway and

moving over near Springfield. This pretty much seals the decision. In a way, it also eases the blow, though there were things that were lost we can never replace." She offered a refill of soft drink around. "How about you and your uncle?"

"We have yet to decide. Scott, what about your family?"

"We haven't decided yet, either. My aunt wants us to move to Joplin near her." He grimaced.

"But you're getting to like this place, right Scott?" Shirley said, drawing a sheepish smile from him.

"Okay, time for staff business." Billie finished off her last slice of pizza and brushed off her hands. "Here's my reason for calling you together. This morning, I visited the sheriff's office to check on a hunch of mine regarding the firestorm. You heard him outline at the briefing how the fire was started–with a lit rope dangling from the train. Well, I asked if there was any portion of the rope remaining and, if so, could I see it. The answer to both questions was yes."

"Oh my God, I know where this is going," Shirley said in anticipation, her eyes wide.

Scott sat forward, dropping his pizza.

Billie nodded. "You got it. It's the same rope stolen from our display."

"Are you sure, Billie?"

"I'm sure. It's too unique, as you well know."

"I can't believe this. Do you think one of those militia guys took it?" Shirley asked. "It was reported lost at about the same time they were meeting."

"Yes, I know, and you said it was a patron who reported it missing. No one else mentioned it?"

"No, and it was a little old lady, one of our regular patrons, who informed me. I'm sure she had nothing to do with its disappearance."

"This happened Monday morning?" Scott asked.

"It would have been sometime over the weekend or Monday morning," Billie answered.

"Then I saw who took it," he calmly said, then sipped his soda.

Billie and Shirley both cast surprised looks at the young man sitting between them.

"Who? When?" Billie urged.

"Sunday afternoon, when Shirley and I came in to work, I was sitting in the basement, going through the gift books, when I heard this car pull up out front of the library. I figured it was someone who was returning some books through the book drop. A minute later I happened to glance out the basement window and saw this man opening his passenger side door. He had a large coil of rope hanging from his arm. He tossed the rope inside. It was a pick-up he was driving. I could tell from the undercarriage."

"Who was it?" Billie asked, her breath catching.

Scott shrugged. "That's the problem. Those basement windows are so narrow, all I could see was the undercarriage, the man's calves and boots, and the rope."

"Scott, why didn't you mention this to me?" Shirley asked, hitting his arm lightly.

"Hey, I thought nothing of it." He blushed slightly. "I guess I was concentrating too much on the gift books to make a connection between the rope in his hand and the rope on the porch. In all honesty, I hadn't paid much attention to it in the first place."

"And you saw nothing, Shirley?" Billie asked.

"Nothing, but now that I think of it, I do recall a car driving up. Like Scott, I probably thought it was someone checking to see if we were open or returning a book."

"The truth is he probably knew we were closed. That's why he came Sunday," Billie said thoughtfully. "You don't remember anything else about him, Scott?"

"My view was only from the calves down."

"The militia guys would have known of the rope," Shirley said.

"This happened on Sunday. They met on Monday," Billie countered.

"But don't forget, they were there days earlier to book the meeting room. They spent some time looking over the place while waiting for you."

"Why would a militia group want to burn down its own camp?" Billie's forehead crinkled. "They must have known it would happen with the loop of fire they were planning–that is, if they did do it."

"Maybe there's nothing down there worth saving. Maybe they don't leave anything behind when they are finished for the day. Maybe they cart it away," Scott said.

"We can't be sure about that."

"They have to be feeling the pressure now," Shirley added. "Especially that leader of theirs who came in to talk to you. Did he leave any clue?"

"No," Billie said, her mind drifting to nothingness for the moment, mostly out of weariness.

She looked out past the screen porch to a large terrace bordering the back of the apartments. The rain had stopped and she could see her uncle playing ball with Buster along a walkway.

"Maybe we should put Scott under hypnosis. It may help him recall a magic identifier," Shirley said in jest.

"You don't recall the make of pickup or license plate?" Billie asked, rejoining the rehash.

"I'm trying to remember. The undercarriage and bumper are all that stick in my mind. The color I don't recall, probably because the truck rode pretty high and I was pretty much looking at it from below. I–wait, wait. There is something I remember..."

"What, Scott–what? Come on, tell us." She leaned forward.

"Yeah, a bumper sticker, a faded one."

"What did it say?" Billie prompted.

"A Friend of...A Friend of...A Friend of the Forest–that's it." He snapped his fingers, a pleased smile crossing his face.

"There you go." Shirley threw her arm wide. "You burn down the forest to prove you are its friend. That's along the lines of burning down a village to save it."

"A Friend of the Forest," Billie repeated.

"You going to pass that along to the sheriff?" Shirley asked.

Billie said nothing.

"Billie, you are going to pass that along to the sheriff, aren't you?"

Chapter Ten

The lumber and stone structures that comprised the ranger station complex, including the main office, garages, storage buildings, and residences, were models of simplicity and utility, Billie noted on entering, a reflection of the depression-era tradition government architects were reluctant to discard. On this occasion she'd decided to call ahead for an appointment, since she carried no information to wield as a wedge.

"Billie Staley to see Mr. Finley," she said to the reception clerk who directed her to an office across the lobby.

"Miss Staley, it's nice to meet you." He greeted her at the door, smoothing back his frizzled, reddish hair. "I understand from the message given me that you were a resident of Woodland Hills?"

"Technically, I suppose I still am," she said, taking the chair he held out for her.

"Sorry, a foolish remark on my part."

"I do appreciate your taking the time to see me."

"What can I do for you?" He seated himself behind his desk.

"I was, or am, the librarian at the Woodland Hills Public library. We were in the middle of a library oral history program at the time the firestorm hit. Are you familiar with oral history programs?"

"Sure am. My father participated in one years ago for a historical society up north." His face lit with remembrance.

"He had all sorts of tales to tell them. I think he used up all their tape."

"One of our participants was a man by the name of Jack Hatch, a former ranger who, I believe, worked in this district. Do you know him?"

"Jack Hatch–can't say I know him." His eyes took on a wary glint. "But I am familiar with him. Why?"

"I was in the middle of an interview with him, when the firestorm struck."

"The library was open?"

"No. I had taped the first portion prior to the fire and would like to conclude it, especially in light of recent events. I think it would be valuable from a historical perspective."

"In what way?" he asked, continuing to conceal any opinion of the man.

"In providing a historical overview of ranger activities in this region. I gather from what he already said at our first meeting there is much to be learned from his personal experiences. Don't you agree?"

"That's very possible."

How come no "Jack's just the guy you should talk to," or "Jack's a legend in ranger circles," or "Jack's a good ol' boy," she wanted to know.

"Was he highly thought of?" she asked, deciding on the direct approach.

"If I didn't know better, I'd think you were a reporter doing a little digging," he remarked, rising to close the interview.

"Nosy me." She determinedly remained seated. "Well, then, let me ask what I primarily came here to ask. Do you know where he resides at present? I have no way of knowing, since our library records have been destroyed."

"Not really. One of our rangers mentioned a while back

that he was living in a cabin over near Mountain Springs. That's about all I know."

And that was about all he was going tell her, she concluded, though she ached to ask more.

She did rise this time. "Thank you, Mr. Finley."

"You're welcome, Miss Staley. Good luck."

A reporter digging up dirt, that was the impression she'd made on him alright, leaving her with the impression there was more dirt to be dug.

Billie drove to the Plainville Public Library and asked if there was an index to local newspaper articles. There wasn't. However, they did have a complete run of the Plainville paper on microfilm. Sitting at a microfilm machine and winding through years of paper was definitely going to be her last resort. Instead, she asked if they kept a clipping file of articles relating to the local area. Fortunately they did, and the librarian led her to the vertical file cabinets where they were housed.

Billie flipped through the manila folders, scanning for subject headings relevant to her search. She settled on "Environment," a folder appearing to contain a surfeit of clippings dating back ten years. Taking it to a table, she browsed the contents, which included countless articles on fire prevention, brush fires, water management, as well as biographical profiles by the dozen. After wading through about five years worth, she came across an article entitled "*Arson Suspected in Ranger Station Fire.*"

The piece described how the early-morning fire started in the interior of the building, causing moderate damage to the structure. According to the Plainville fire chief, there was no evidence of breaking and entering. Despite this, the chief of the Forest Service speculated it was either the work of "neo-terrorists" or "anti-government locals."

A second article under the title "*House Razed by Fire*," dated six months later, also caught her interest. It related how a fire of unknown origin destroyed the home of Jack Hatch, a Richfield resident and Forest Service employee. Hatch's wife and two children, the article stated, were not home at the time of the blaze. An investigation into the cause of the fire was under way. She searched the folder's remaining clippings for follow-up articles to the two incidents but could find none.

A victim of a terrorist act against his home and family. A long and troubled relationship with his employer. A bumper sticker bearing a "Friend of the Forest" message. It all added up. However, before she reported back to the sheriff, she decided on one final bold stroke to seal her case.

Before leaving the library, Billie checked a state road map for Mountain Springs. It was a forty-five minute drive. Along the way, she stopped to purchase a small tape recorder, which she tucked in her purse.

Mountain Springs was even smaller than pre-firestorm Woodland Hills, tiny enough not to have a public library but large enough to boast a general store. She entered the store and began to browse, noting in the corner a burly man with a moon-shaped face and bull neck she took to be the proprietor. He was halfway up a ladder, meticulously taking inventory when he paused in his counting of cereal boxes to acknowledge her presence, flashing a welcoming smile.

"Excuse me, sir. May I interrupt you for a moment?"

"Yes, ma'am, what can I help you with?" he asked, swaying his ample backside down the ladder.

"Do you by chance know of a man by the name of Jack Hatch who lives in this area?"

"I know everyone who lives in this area. They all pass

through here at one time or another, including Jack Hatch. Where do you know him from?"

"We were in a history program together at the Woodland Hills Public Library."

"You from Woodland Hills?"

"Yes."

He shook his head in sympathy. "Man, you people took it on the chin, didn't you?"

"Yes, we did. Could you tell me where Mr. Hatch lives?"

He walked to a large floor cooler placed between some fishing gear and souvenirs, lifted the lid, rolled up his shirt sleeve, and doggedly worked his hand through some chunks of ice, before pulling out a soft drink can. "Lemonade. Want one?"

"No thank you."

"You goin' alone?" he asked, taking a swig of the drink.

"Yes. Why?"

"Nothing. None of my business. I've only been by his place once or twice. If I remember right, you continue on the blacktop road you came in on for about another mile where you'll see a deer-crossing sign. About a hundred yards past the sign you'll see a dirt road. There's no street marker, so you'll have to be on the lookout for it or you'll miss the dang thing. Go up the road a half mile or so and you'll see to your left a cabin sitting a hundred yards into the woods. It's barely visible from the road."

Billie found the deer-crossing sign and dirt road and was negotiating a series of deep ruts, when she caught a glimpse of the cabin situated on a small rise behind a stand of trees. She followed a grooved path leading up to the structure, which from its exterior did not appear much different from her uncle's cabin. Slowing to a stop, she noticed a makeshift carport had been attached to the rear of the unit. A pickup was parked inside.

Before she could conduct a quick inspection of its bumper, the cabin's screen door swung open and out stepped Mr. Hatch onto the porch to check on his visitor. The look on his face was neither one of surprise or disappointment, only indifference.

"Hello, Mr. Hatch."

"Hello, Miss Staley."

"I hope you don't mind me showing up unannounced like this," she said, approaching a pile of curved hand-cut rocks that served as porch steps.

"How did you find me?"

"A couple of people told me you lived up this way. If you recall, today is the day we were scheduled to complete your oral history session. With what's happened, I thought it would be important to finish your segment, if you have the time."

"For what purpose? There's no library left."

"That's the point. This will be the seminal event in the town's history. Now more than ever, the story must be told, while it's fresh, if only for posterity's sake."

"Come on in," he said, again revealing little emotion or reaction.

Despite her determination, an uneasiness accompanied her on entering his home alone.

It was a two-room cabin with oak flooring, a loft, bunk alcove, gaslights, rocking chair, and two wood stoves, one for heating and the one in the kitchen for both cooking and heating. The entire cabin was in semi-disarray with empty food containers scattered about on counters and tables. An odor of tobacco permeated the place.

"Have a chair," he said, pointing to a worn wooden dining

table, its surface bare, except for an overflowing tin ashtray and lighter.

She casually pulled out the tape recorder from her purse and set it on the table.

"Ready," she asked.

He shrugged his shoulders, still perplexed by her appearance, no doubt.

"At the close of our last session, you were mentioning some of the difficulties you were having with some of the locals and your supervisors. Perhaps you could pick up there," she said, punching on the recorder.

He looked hard at her, as though unsure of his interest in continuing. "Weren't the previous tapes destroyed in the fire?"

"No, I had them in my personal possession," she lied.

"You have a new recorder."

"Yes, it's of much better quality."

"Mind if I smoke? One of the many bad habits I've picked up since my Forest Service days."

"No," she lied again.

He slipped a near-empty pack from his shirt pocket, jacked up a remaining cigarette, and lit it, discharging the first drag into the already fouled air.

"It became a personal matter," he started back on his story, rubbing at the stubble on his chin. "Vandals began to set fires to Forest Service trucks, spray-paint graffiti on the ranger station walls, and strew nails on the driveway."

"Was there any reaction from law enforcement authorities?"

"Not much. They couldn't get any cooperation from the residents. The ones who did report them had their cattle shot, pets killed, or property burned."

"You said they set fires to Forest Service trucks. Did they

attempt to burn the ranger station itself?"

"Somebody did. What was strange was that the fire was set from inside of the building."

"How did they get in?"

"That's just it. There was no evidence of breaking or entering. Therefore, they couldn't rule out the possibility it was an inside job, and since I was their favorite whipping boy, I was the one looked at with suspicion."

She straightened in her chair. "They never solved it?"

"No. The investigators decided it was some type of incendiary device that was brought in. The bottom line is the case was never solved, which meant I was left hanging under a cloud of suspicion. At that point, I was getting it from all sides–from my supervisors, from the locals, from the environmentalists, and from the recreationists."

"Why were the recreation people upset?"

"We were cutting off forest roads to preserve wildlife, for one thing. There were other issues they would raise at public meetings. They never missed an opportunity to bitch."

"Yet, you stayed on."

"Yes, but then things really got personal."

"In what way?"

"Instead of spreading nails and spraying graffiti, they burned down my house." He waved his cigarette in anger. "I'd call that personal."

"They?"

"Probably the locals. It was never determined, though it made me more determined. If they were going to break the law, I was sure as hell going to enforce it. I was prepared to take them to court at every turn. That's when the Forest Service higher-ups started to lean on me. They said I was becoming too intense and that the department's efforts to build bridges with the community were being undermined by my activities. Suddenly, supervisors were dropping hints about me taking early retirement."

"Do you have a family?"

"Yes," he sighed, blowing another puff of smoke into the air, "or at least I did have a wife and two sons."

"Where are they now?"

"California. Our house being torched was the final straw. My wife got fed up. Said it was no way to raise a family. She was right. The irony was that the kids loved the outdoors. We would go on long hikes, take float trips down the rivers, go fishing. Our family felt at home roaming these woods. The indoor life turned out to be the real problem for us. Kids at school would taunt my sons about their ranger father. My wife was getting the same from some of the neighbors."

"You decided to stay?"

"As strange as it may seem, yes. Like I said, I was determined to see it through. The one word that would appear over and over on my job evaluations was "dedicated." I loved my job and most of all, understood it better than anyone else. I know the forest and I know what it takes to keep it growing. The fact is Forest Service personnel don't often get to see the fruits of their labors. Trees grow slowly and, consequently, changes in the forest come gradually. The work demands patience. However, my supervisors could only hear the complaining, so they caved. They called me in and said it was time to go, to either take a desk job or early retirement. I chose neither and got fired. I could have raised a stink, but didn't. If someone doesn't want me to work for them, then the feeling becomes mutual."

He flicked an ash into the tray and awaited her next question.

Sounded to her like he'd valued his job above his family. "Why didn't you join your family?"

"I originally intended to. I thought I would work a while longer, and then, if things settled down, take the early retirement and join them. Things didn't settle down, however, and while I was battling away here, my wife found another man there and ended up filing for a divorce." He took a last drag on his cigarette, snuffed it out, and lit another.

She grimaced slightly, the stench of the tobacco threatening to interfere with her thought process. Could it be failed rangers took to tobacco the way failed cops took to booze?

"I'll ask again. Despite it all, you remain?"

"Yeah, I remain. I lost a job and a family and yet I remain, because I believe in the old notion of retribution."

"How so?" she asked, alerted by his reference.

"That evil done is ultimately punished."

She squirmed in her chair. "By a divine hand, I assume you mean."

"Divine or human."

"You mentioned at the last session that you organized a Friend of the Forest program. Did you have much success with it?"

"A little, but not enough to turn the tide of local opinion."

"How did you market the program to the community?"

He scratched his chin again, watching her more intently. "Public service announcements, public meetings, flyers, the usual stuff."

"Bumper stickers?"

"Yes, bumper stickers also. Why?"

"I've seen a few around. Do you have one?"

"For you?" he asked incredulously.

"No, I mean do you have one on your truck?"

He glared at her for a moment, doused his half-finished cigarette, and reached over to punch off the recorder with a whack of his fist, catching her by surprise. She jumped.

"Listen here, lady. This may have started out as an oral history session, but something tells me it has turned into a creature of another color. For one thing, your coming all the way out here before the ash has settled. Secondly, to ask this line of questioning which leaves me to wonder what the hell you're driving at."

She took a deep breath, then barged right in. "Someone who stole a display rope from the library, the rope used in starting the Woodland Hills firestorm, had a 'Friend of the Forest' sticker on his truck bumper."

"I see. It's not an oral history session, after all. It's an interrogation." His eyes reddened from either the smoke or her audacity, she wasn't sure.

"What, did the sheriff send you?" he continued. "How clever of him—we can lure a confession out of him and there's no need to have a lawyer looking over our shoulder to remind him of his rights. No, I hate to spoil your strategy, but I didn't take your rope, nor did I start the fire. I'm the one with the record of putting fires out, remember?"

"I'm sorry, Mr. Hatch." She scooted her chair backward a bit, nervous about the anger she'd aroused. "I hope you understand my wanting to clear this up. It was our rope that was used to destroy our library. I felt a duty to check it out."

"To play a little detective, you mean. You need to take a breather lady. You know, the way you were handling that oral history class, I was beginning to believe you were a woman wise beyond your years. Now I'm not so sure about the wise part. I'm thinking, maybe you should let the years catch up with you." He glared at her, but stayed on his side of the table. "By the way, that rope trick is an old one for arsonists. They used to tie them to horse saddles and drag them around to start brush fires. No, you're barking up the wrong tree, Miss Staley. You want to know the one you should be barking up?"

"Which one's that?" she asked, muting her curiosity, lest she end up looking more foolish. *Do you have one on your truck?* How stupid was it of her to ask such a question!

"The railroad tree. They are responsible for keeping the track beds clear of brush, which they did a poor job of doing when I was there. They're required to clear them of dead leaves, dead grass, dry brush, and any other inflammable substance to a point two hundred feet distant from the center of the tracks. They also are required to post warning placards supplied by us, which they never got around to doing. That's the letter of the law." He thumped his finger on the table. "I was on their case all the time over it. The bottom line is they are liable for damages to persons whose property is injured or destroyed by a fire started by a train. And not only are they liable to residents, they're liable to the local government for any expenses incurred in fighting the fire. Those are going to amount to pretty big damages, wouldn't you say?"

She shook her head in confusion. "Why would they set the fire?"

"Who said it was deliberate?"

"The sheriff said it was."

"Based on what the train crew told him, no doubt."

"You mean it could have been an accident?" The thought never occurred to her. "I don't get it."

"Talk to a railroad man. I'm finished talking," he said, pushing his chair roughly back, "except to tell you to take a look at my bumpers on your way out."

She did, and they were clean, and she was thankful—thankful she hadn't gone to the sheriff first with her clever little plan.

Billie was back on the big road, as the locals liked to call it, the main highway leading to and intersecting Woodland Hills...or what remained of it. In the distance the neon appendage to the Buzzard's Roost Saloon appeared on the horizon. At once, she turned her attention to the roadside for a marker and access road she knew would be approaching. On seeing it, she eased onto a narrow gravel path hemmed by rows of trees untouched by the firestorm that had wreaked its fury only a few miles to the west.

About a mile down the path she passed three middle-aged men jogging alongside the road, their shirts and shorts drenched with sweat, their eyes glued to the ground, paying her no heed as she passed them by. Further down she crossed a small creek and entered a large clearing in the middle of which stood a cinderblock building adjoined by two wooden structures she took to be guesthouses. A third, smaller facility fronted the main building. A sign indicated it to be a reception area. Further into the clearing she arrived at a fork in the road, its two branches forming a lengthy circular drive leading to the entrance of the complex.

She slowed the truck, conscious of the loud crunching of gravel announcing her arrival. She eased to the side of the road, her vehicle the sole one in sight. The silence was now total, as large and full as the forest, pierced only by the cackle of a crow.

Hopping from the truck, she approached the entry door. A simple "enter" sign was mounted on its front. She paused before opening it, concerned she might be violating a privacy.

It was a needless concern for the lobby was deserted. They must be at prayer services, she concluded.

She took a moment to sign a guest register, noting she was thus far the only registrant of the day. To her right was a small opened room marked gift shop, to her left a chapel with closed door. Fueled by curiosity as much as her reason for being there, she opened the chapel door and was greeted by a life-size crucifix towering high above a massive stone altar framed by mahogany walls, a skylight, and two large, rose-tinted stained-glass windows. A faint odor of incense permeated the room.

She slipped into a back pew, one of six facing the altar. At the moment, she felt as though she'd stepped off of life's merry-go-round. A break was in order, no doubt about it, before she boarded again. Hatch was right. She needed to take a breather, clear her head, and not get ahead of herself. She could have added to his admonition the need to salve her wounded ego.

Billie sat in silence for nearly an hour, until the creak of a door located behind the altar drew her attention to a young man of short stature with kidney-shaped eyes and dark, half-moon eyebrows entering the room. Of Southeast Asian extraction and a long way from his ancestral home, she assumed. That's where she wanted to be—a world apart. He gave her a glance, along with a pious nod, and proceeded to retrieve a chalice from a gilded tabernacle adorning the altar before departing.

Alone once more, she attempted again to focus her thoughts on what was important in her life. You feel how you think, she always believed, though she soon found herself trying not to think at all, as if the process itself precluded a peace of mind. Was this simply a way of avoiding responsibilities and the trouble that flowed from them? In the end, wasn't responsibility the price you paid for joining the human condition?

She ended her meditation, her mind in mid-stream. Upon leaving she decided to pay a quick visit to the gift shop. On display were articles ranging from carved wooden crosses and rosaries to prayer cards featuring the hand of a gifted calligrapher, perhaps belonging to one of the monks. Attached to one wall of the room were metal shelves, neatly stacked with tin receptacles containing the fruitcakes Cory had mentioned. Everything was in precise order, a reflection of the orderliness of the monastic world.

If only that order could be brought back into her own life, she thought, as she continued to scan the room. She noticed in a corner a small cash deposit box with a price list posted above it for visitors to make payment for their purchases. Wishing to make some kind of contribution, she decided to purchase one of the fruitcakes. In reaching for one, she determined it must have been a taller monk who was assigned to shelve them, for it required her to stretch to the tip of her toes to retrieve it.

Unfortunately, she momentarily lost her balance while grabbing hold of one of the containers, causing the entire pile and the pile next to it to crumble. As she dodged the avalanche, cans tumbled to the marble floor, shattering the silence with a staccato of clangs she was sure could be heard throughout the complex. One container rolled on its side and out the door, eventually teetering into a death spiral, each noisy spin and whirl heightening her anxiety.

She scrambled to restore the containers to their proper place on the shelves, again having to struggle with her reach to do so. Thankfully, a cursory inspection of each can revealed no major denting. She had all in order, when she recalled the one in the foyer. She turned to retrieve it but was met at the door by a monk cradling it in the palms of his hands, in much the same pose as the monk portrayed on the lid of the container.

"Sorry, I had an accident," she said demurely.

He was dressed in a gray robe that matched the gray wisps of hair falling across his forehead. Clear blue eyes gleamed from a weathered face wreathed with a smile.

"I seem to have a knack for bringing disorder to order," she added.

"But things appear to be back in order," he said, extending his arm to return the remaining container to its proper place.

"Wait," she said. "I would like to buy one."

She rummaged from her purse the proper cash and deposited it into the money box.

"Brother Luke," he said, offering her his hand.

"Billie," she replied, accepting his warm clasp.

"Is this your first visit?" he asked courteously, handing her the container.

"Yes. I heard of the place, the monastery, I mean, from a friend and decided to make a visit. I guess I was trying to withdraw from all the hubbub for a few minutes."

"Oh yes, we have guests who withdraw for minutes at a time, some who withdraw for a day, some for a week, and some even for a lifetime," he replied, motioning to his garb.

"May I ask–how long have you been a resident here?"

"Close to thirty years, I believe. Time is not a priority here, so keeping precise track of it is not a pressing matter."

"Well, I should be going," she said, somewhat reluctantly. "Again, I apologize for the mess I made."

"No problem. You fixed it. That's one thing the monastic life and the secular life have in common. You have a problem, you have to fix it. There's little contemplating to be done," he said with a wise sparkle in his eye.

"Oh, may I ask you one more off-the-wall question, now that I've knocked just about everything else off the wall."

"Sure," he said, widening his smile in anticipation.

"How did you come to know you belonged here?"

"How did I come to know I belonged here?" he repeated thoughtfully. "I would say it was when I stopped my searching. That's when I knew I belonged here. I was a wanderer in my youth, a sojourner, until I reached this community. Others may say it was when I stopped dreaming. But, yes, I would say it was when I stopped looking. Why do you ask?"

Why indeed? She paused, assessing her words, then, "I've always considered it a personal achievement to feel a sense of belonging."

She returned to the truck, stopping to gaze up at the cliffs from where not so long ago she'd looked down on the very spot she now stood. Shading her eyes with the container, she was able to make out the figure of a man on a horse at the edge of the cliff, undoubtedly surveying the scene below him.

Was he able to see her? How could he know it was her? After all, she was driving her uncle's pickup.

Suddenly, a shaft of bright light appeared in her vision. Realizing it was a reflection of the sun off the container, she yanked it down.

"Nice going, Billie," she whispered to herself. "You couldn't have done a better job of calling attention to yourself." She held her gaze, while the figure on the horse held his position.

Who would make the first move was an issue she did not care to pursue. She turned and headed for the truck and the big road beyond.

"Uncle Ray, I'm over here at this garage where they towed my truck. They tell me the damage is worth more than the truck."

"Will your insurance pay?"

"I called them and they said to get a couple of estimates. It sounded as if they would."

"What about your personal belongings?"

"They were nearly totaled, also. I did manage to salvage a few items. The family photos and mementos, they...they..."

"Listen, Billie. I know it may not be the same, but I have plenty of family photos stashed away that I managed to get out, including some of your parents. You can take your pick of those."

"It also looks like I may have to borrow your truck, until the insurance money comes through."

"No problem."

"Okay, I'm going to stop by the town library for a while and then I'll be home. And, Uncle Ray, could you do me a favor? Ask Shirley and Scott if they could stop over around seven tonight. I'd like for you to be there, too."

"For leftover pizza?"

"And fruitcake," she added.

"And fruitcake—now there's a combination," he replied, as if he'd come to fully expect that from her.

Back at the Plainville Library, Billie scanned the public access computer for news stories on the firestorm, concentrating on items relating to the rail line and its crew. Other than a brief reference or two, their role for the most part was ignored in the accounts. Having reached a point of diminishing returns, she decided on a new tack. With a few twists of search terms, she was successful in calling up the home page of the Missouri Valley Railroad Corporation, the freight line referred to in the news stories as the one involved in the incident. Included in a streamer of icons running down the left-hand side of the page was one for current news.

She clicked on it and instantly a line of headlines scrolled onto the screen. Her gaze was immediately drawn to the one reading "*Train Crew Praised for Quick Reaction in Forest Fire.*" She called the article up and discovered it to be not only brief but also a rehash of general news accounts, except for the opening paragraph, which highlighted the crew's alerting of authorities to the conflagration.

There was one more thing. At the close of the article appeared a snapshot of the crew's members, the downloading of which she watched with a mixture of initial interest and subsequent surprise.

What a wonderful advance in the world of information retrieval, she thought upon leaving, the availability of computers in libraries.

Chapter Eleven

"You didn't go to the sheriff?" Shirley asked in disbelief.

"The information I had was incomplete."

"Incomplete?" Her mouth dropped open. "Scott saw the sticker, he saw what it said, he saw the guy taking the rope, he saw he drove a truck. What else do you need?"

"Everyone around here drives a truck," she answered, watching the reaction of Shirley, Uncle Ray, and Scott as they sat around the small kitchen table in her apartment, an empty box of pizza on the table between them.

"Not me," Shirley retorted with a pinch of pride.

"I wanted to talk to you again, before I took that step. Uncle Ray, what's the job of the train crew? Are there normally three to a crew?"

He nodded. "It's getting down to that. Not long ago, five were required to be on a freight train, but the railroads have been trying to cut back on labor costs to save money. Those kinds of moves don't make for a happy union."

"So, if this was a crew of three, it would be comprised of what, an engineer and who else?"

"A conductor and brakeman, most likely," he answered, pinching off another piece of fruitcake. He was the only one who'd touch it.

"The conductor does what?" she asked.

"Conducts," snapped Scott, grinning.

Billie tossed him a narrowed gaze.

"He keeps records of each carload," Uncle Ray answered.

187

"He also can carry out the duties of the brakeman and switchman, if he needs to. Generally, he oversees the entire operation."

"And the brakeman?"

"He watches out for smoke, sparks, and other signs of sticking brakes–the hot boxes."

"What's a hot box?" Scott asked, beating her to the question.

"Overheated axle bearings. They can produce a cloud of smoke, which the crew up front of the train can easily miss. That's his main job. He also can spot broken air brakes. If it wasn't for him, someone would have to trudge all the way back from the engine to do the checking."

"And where is the conductor stationed?" She persisted. The answer was here somewhere.

"Any place the guy wants to be." He waved a hand. "As I said, he directs the whole operation. Remember too, communications have improved. They now carry hand held radios."

"Okay, if this train had a crew of three, two could have been riding up front in the engine cab and one in the back, right?"

"If the one in the back had something to ride in. Otherwise, all three could be in the front."

"Like a caboose," she said.

"Yes."

"Oh, those cute little cars at the end of the train," Shirley said. "You don't see many of them anymore. I always remember someone waving from inside it as we sat at a railroad crossing and waited for it to come by."

"You want to buy one?" Scott asked.

"Buy one?" Shirley looked bemused.

"Yeah. People buy them," Scott said. "Like rail passenger cars, they turn them into antique stores or classrooms or other stationary structures."

"To answer you question, Billie," her uncle resumed, with a drawn out sigh, "there are still some in operation, but many are bein' phased out with the cutbacks in the crew sizes. Again, it's all a matter of money. The caboose has costs connected with its operation, like electrical, sewage, food and water, and maintenance. I've seen members of a crew turn a caboose into a combination apartment-garage. The bottom line is there's no sense in havin' it if there are no crew members along to ride it."

"Let's assume there was a caboose. That would mean the engineer and conductor were up front and the brakeman in the back."

"Good possibility," her uncle nodded.

"I understand it's the responsibility of the railroad to clear the dry underbrush from the tracks. Why is that?"

"Sparks from the train can set the stuff on fire."

"Sparks caused by what?" She leaned forward in her seat. Now they were getting somewhere. "The hot boxes?"

"Yes, and by the normal friction of a wheel against the rail. A locked wheel also will spin off sparks."

"Especially if it's trying to negotiate a sharp bend?"

"Yes."

"Lots of sparks?" she asked.

"Showers of them, particularly if they're comin' from a locked wheel."

"Wait a minute," Shirley held up a hand. "You're not suggesting sparks set off this fire? I thought the sheriff said it was the lit rope."

"She's right, Billie. That's what the sheriff said," Scott nodded.

"He said it based on what the crew or a member of the crew told him, I'm sure of that, which brings me to the point of why I wanted to talk to you." She reached for her purse. "Today, I went to the Plainville Public Library to do some research. Here's what I discovered."

She pulled out a sheet of paper with the downloaded image of the train crew and held it face out to the group.

"Oh, my God," Shirley said, putting palm to mouth.

"I don't recognize any of them," Scott said.

Her uncle agreed.

"It's the militia guy who booked the meeting room," Shirley said, her gaze glued to the photo.

"The square-shouldered one who I originally thought was their leader," Billie said, pointing to the picture. "According to the caption here, his name is Al Munford and he was the brakeman on the train."

"So…it was the militia, after all." Scott's eyes widened.

"It means there's a militia connection, but I'm not sure he set the fire."

"What do you mean?" Shirley asked.

"Why set a fire from a train run by a railroad you work for, a train you happen to be assigned to. It's not exactly a way to ensure anonymity."

"It certainly was convenient, though," Scott said.

"And why there, when you know there's a good chance it's going to wipe out your camp?"

"Maybe he got into a squabble with them," her uncle volunteered.

"No, the anonymity is too important. Let me pose another theory to you." She eyed them speculatively.

"Okay, Miss Gumshoe, let's hear it," Shirley cracked, leaning back in her chair and crossing her feet on a footstool.

"It has to do with what Uncle Ray said. Suppose a wheel did lock on the train, or friction of the normal kind occurred on the long turn, sending sparks flying, igniting the underbrush. And suppose you're the brakeman stationed in the caboose and for some reason, you miss the fireworks. Maybe, you're asleep, or reading, or whatever, and you become aware of the situation too late. The fires already have begun to build out of control. Perhaps the engineer or conductor spots what's happening from the front of the train and radios back to find out what's going on. The train is stopped for you to check. You suddenly realize you've goofed up big time, that your job could be in jeopardy." She looked to her uncle. "Right, Uncle Ray?"

"I'd say so," he replied.

"So, you begin to think of the consequences and devise a way to cover your rear. You grab the rope you have in the caboose, soak it with some fuel you have stored there, tie it to the side of a rear car, and call for the conductor to come back. By the time he makes the walk back, you have a reason for pointing the finger of blame elsewhere. You show the burning rope to him and he says let's get out of here, blowing his whistle and calling the authorities at the same time." She finished in triumph.

"How do you know he was the one who took the rope?" Shirley asked.

"That's the missing link," she responded, tapping her finger on the table absentmindedly.

"Don't you think the sheriff's investigators checked into the possibility of it being a crew member?" her uncle asked.

"I don't believe they gave it serious consideration. I think they took the crew's word at face value when they talked to them. After all, there was the burned rope right before their eyes, a favorite tactic of arsonists. Also, don't forget the direct calls coming into fire officials' offices from the two members of the crew stationed up front. I'm sure they were reporting exactly what they were seeing and what they were being told by the brakeman." She shook her head. "No, the investigators had no reason at all to suspect the crew or a crew member at the time."

"What if they were all in on it?" Scott asked.

"A possibility, but I'm betting not. Why would they either want to set the fire or cover for the brakeman whose responsibility it was to detect such conditions?"

"Why would he take the rope on board in the first place?" Shirley's brow furrowed, as if trying to sort it all out.

"Uncle Ray just said it was not unusual for a crew member to turn a caboose into a garage, so I don't believe it would be out of the ordinary for him to store a rope there. People use rope for any number of reasons, right?" she asked, scanning the faces in the room.

"He could have been using it to clean his engine oil," her uncle said.

"Cleaning his engine oil?" Shirley asked.

"It's somethin' people used to do during hard times. They still do, if they're short on cash. In case you don't know, the engine oil you put in your car does not wear out, though it gets contaminated with all kinds of residue from the combustion process and all those additives people throw into it."

"They clean it with a rope?" Scott asked.

"Sure do. They take a clean piece of natural rope, usually made of cotton, and two large glass containers and set up a little recycling station. They put the container filled with the used oil on a top shelf and the empty container on a lower one and place the ends of the rope clear to the bottom of each jug, forming a hoop. The oil then crawls up the rope through–what

192

do you call it? Capillary action, and then starts down it again toward the empty container. As the oil passes through the fibers, the contaminants are trapped. At first, the oil flows slowly, but once the effect of gravity kicks in, it starts to travel faster, though it takes a couple of weeks for all the oil to seep to the bottom container."

"And you think he was doing this on the caboose?" Shirley asked.

"Could have been," her uncle replied.

"That would explain how he already had a soaked rope available," Scott said.

"Except the sheriff said the rope was soaked in gasoline. He also told me it was made from Manila, the strongest kind of natural fiber," Billie said, pouring doubt on her uncle's suggestion. "Furthermore, I don't think Munford is the sort to be pinching pennies."

"Then maybe that wasn't what he was doin'," her uncle responded, reaching for the last bit of cake. "You were askin' what he could have been doin' with it and all I was doin' was givin' you an example. For all I know, he could have been jumpin' rope to pass the time."

"Too long a rope," Shirley quipped.

"Like he couldn't cut it," Scott said.

"Okay, okay." Billie wagged her finger at them. "The important thing is he had it with him, for whatever reason. He undoubtedly saw it the first time he was hanging around the library, waiting to book the meeting room. He may have thought it was a handy item to have on his caboose and decided to grab it at a later time–which reminds me, Scott, you said the sticker on the truck was faded and scratched, right?"

"Yes, like somebody had started to take it off and then gave up."

"Knowing if that was his truck is all we need to seal the connection," she said.

"You are going to take this information to the sheriff, aren't you, Billie?" Shirley asked.

She didn't answer, her mind busy contemplating the possibilities.

"Billie! You are going to pass this on to the sheriff, aren't you?" her uncle asked more forcefully, as if he meant to make sure she did.

"Yes, I plan on passing it on–if only I had the final connection to bring to him," she added as an afterthought.

Al Munford lived on the 3800 block of Euclid Avenue in Poplar Bluff, the second house from the corner. She was parked in front the third house, the front bumper of his truck framed in her rearview mirror.

The elm-lined street was a mix of A-frame single-family homes and brick duplexes set back a good distance from the street. The sleepy scene was broken only by the distant sound of children at play coming from a small playground at the far end of the avenue. She couldn't help but wonder if any of the youngsters answered to the name Munford.

Taking a deep breath, she hopped from her truck, paused to let a sidewalk bicyclist pass, walked to a welcome mat as worn and torn as the Friend-of-the-Forest sticker on his truck bumper, and pressed the doorbell. A moment later, Munford's frame was filling the doorway, his lackadaisical manner indicating he didn't recognize her, but his eyes revealing otherwise.

"Mr. Munford, perhaps you remember me. I'm Billie Staley, the librarian from the Woodland Hills public library."

"Jesus, what the hell are you doing here?" he said, the

cockiness he'd displayed in the parking lot presently replaced by wariness.

"'I've come to get the rope back you took from the library."

He stepped outside, slamming the door shut behind him. "What the hell are you talkin' about, woman?"

"I'm sure you saw the large rope that was a part of our porch display the day you came to book the meeting room. It's missing."

"What makes you think I took it?"

"One of our staff members saw you take it." She clinched her fingers until her nails bit into her palms.

"Is that right? And you came all the way over here to tell me this?"

"You came all the way over there to take it. I just wanted to give you the opportunity to return it, before I turned the matter over to the sheriff."

"You're going to call the sheriff in over a missing piece of rope?" His voice grew louder.

"If need be."

"By God, you're serious, aren't you?"

"Yes."

She noticed him stiffen a bit, before blinking.

"Okay, so what if I took your rope. How much do you want for it?"

"I'd rather have the rope back."

"I don't have it anymore."

"What happened to it?"

"For Christ's sake, lady, what difference does it make? Here. Here's twenty bucks I'll give you for the damn thing," he said, pulling a bill from his wallet. "That should cover it."

"I'm curious," she said, taking the bill and placing it in her purse. "Just what were you planning on doing with the rope?"

"Let me put it this way," he said, leaning his face into hers. "My original plans for it kind of went astray, but it still came in mighty handy for me."

"I'm sure it did," she replied.

"You going to take that money and start a new library," he asked, his cockiness fully restored. "We got a nice one here you can use."

"Yes, I know, with a nice meeting room. You should patronize it more often, instead of looking elsewhere."

"You need to go back to tracking down overdue library books, woman. Oh, I forgot, you don't have any books left to track down. Well, maybe that twenty will get you started again." He looked her over, much as his friends had done that day earlier. "Yeah, you got a lot of brass coming over here. I'll hand that to you. I'd have thought the parking lot session would have taught you to tread lightly. Jesus, coming over here all sure of yourself, all on account of a piece of rope."

"This time I was sure of myself."

"How's that?"

"This time I made sure. I went to the sheriff first," she said softly, as much to herself as to him.

"What—"

His eyes veered over her shoulder to the two men she knew would be striding up the sidewalk at any moment.

"Mr. Munford," Sheriff Booker stepped beside her. "This is Deputy Carlson, our lead investigator into the Woodland Hills fire. I believe you two have met."

Munford inched backward toward his closed door. "What's going on here?"

"We made a mistake in our investigation, Mr. Munford," the sheriff said, "mostly due to what you told us and your fellow crew members. All along, we were looking outside the train for evidence instead of inside it. We talked to the engineer and conductor again and did some checking of that caboose and the train wheels. What we found were particles of that rope, many of them, and the fuel used to soak it in. We also found evidence of a faulty train wheel. The railroad has been notified."

"I did not set that fire." His gaze shifted, as if looking for escape.

"No, you didn't set the fire," Sheriff Booker agreed, reaching for his handcuffs. "Nonetheless, you are being charged with criminal negligence and obstruction of justice, in addition to any other appropriate charges the prosecutor may decide on down the line."

Billie walked to the sheriff's truck as they began to read Mr. Munford his rights. A female deputy helped her remove the wire strapped to her chest. She started to walk back to her truck but quickly reversed her footsteps, handing to the deputy a twenty-dollar bill.

Chapter Twelve

Though the haze in the sky and smell of smoke in the air had waned, the blanket of ash remained, a reminder of a cycle of the wild familiar to stewards of forests past and present.

On this morning the air was cool and the sun bright, its beams breathing a life back into the scarred landscape. Revisiting the scene, Billie easily could envision Mr. Whitington's stately card catalog standing proud inside the refurbished old mill, its existence, unlike that of the forest, immune to renewal. Her instinct was to find the humor in it, ease the pain by making light of it. With time, she could.

She walked the perimeter of the burned out building, examining the rubble with the devotion of a crime scene investigator, stooping to finger the flakes of ash, standing where the porch stood, sitting on a slag of metal where her office had been. Was this the stuff of an oral history that one day would be asked of her?

One didn't survive the ordeal she'd been through without changing, deepening, one's view of life.

Billie mused a while before ambling off to the river's edge to await the approaching figure she glimpsed from the corner of her eye.

"Hello, Billie."

"Hello, Cory."

"I thought I might find you here. I checked just about everywhere else."

"I was waiting for my uncle. He's up the road, taking a

last look at his old place."

"Last look?" He leaned back on his booted heels, his hands thrust in his back jean pockets. "Does that mean you're leaving?"

"Yes."

He toed at the ground with his right boot, like a restless stallion. "Listen, Billie, I'm telling you right when I say our organization had nothing to do with this. That Munford guy was someone new. He was acting on his own."

"I believe you," she said, reaching down to stroke the tranquil water.

"Every outfit has its misfits. We just need to do a better job of spotting ours."

She said nothing, continuing her caressing of the water, her eyes drawn to the path of the river, as it drifted purposely downstream–to what end?

"It merges with the Current River," he said, his eyes tracking hers. "They make a good couple, though there's a bit of rough water at their meeting point."

She recalled how her father once likened a marriage to the confluence of two determined rivers, joined to a common goal. She had her answer.

"We had some fun out there on the trail, didn't we?" he said, breaking a brief silence.

"Yes, we did."

"You know, I was beginning to believe we had a future together. I thought you might be the one I'd been waiting for." He watched her steadily, hope still lingering in the depth of his gaze.

She stood, brushing the water off her hand. "It's hard to build a future, Cory, when the past is colliding."

"Then why not throw away the past and just think of the

future. We could do that, you know," he said in earnest. "All it takes is some determination. We both got plenty of that."

"We can no more throw away the past, Cory, than Mr. Whitington could throw away his card catalog."

"What? Catalog?" He hunched his shoulders. "I don't understand."

"Nothing. I hope the right woman crosses your path some day, Cory. I do," she trailed off, glimpsing her uncle's truck rolling down the road trailing a cloud of ash, and watching it pull to a stop a short distance away.

"Goodbye, Cory. It was nice meeting you," she said, holding out her hand.

"Nice meeting you, Billie." He accepted it, a somber look of reality overtaking the concern on his face.

She walked briskly to her uncle's truck, hopped into the cab, and fought off Buster's affections.

"Is that the Cory fellow?" Uncle Ray asked.

"That's the Cory fellow," she said.

"Damn nice-lookin' guy," he said, turning the ignition.

She nodded, her gaze firmly focused on the forward view.

Another ending, soon to be followed by another beginning, and perhaps another lesson or two to be learned along the way.

Epilogue

June 1999

"I got a letter from Shirley," Billie said, waving it to her husband sitting across the living room.

"Shirley who?" he asked, looking up from a book on old books he was reading.

"Shirley Bennington, the woman I used to work with in Woodland Hills."

"Oh, what's she up to?"

"She and her husband are now living in Springfield. She's working in the public library system there as a coordinator of volunteers. I suppose you don't recall Scott McKinley either, the kid who also worked there with me?"

"Vaguely."

"He ended up going to school at the University of Missouri. Apparently, he decided Ozarks State College, where he started, wasn't for him. Shirley says he later dropped out of MU to start an automotive restoration business outside of Kansas City. I'll have to show this to Uncle Ray when he gets back from his fishing trip."

"Needless to say, I'm glad you decided to stick to your career path," her husband said with a warm smile, before returning his attention to his book.

Yes, she had decided to stick with it, accepting a job offer from the state library as a computer consultant, on the recommendation of Chad Jenkins, no less. She then convinced her uncle to move with her to a lakefront home on the northern arm of the Lake of the Ozarks, an hour's drive from her office in Jefferson City. By that time, they both were of a mind to stay put. The nomad within her was no more, or at least not kicking.

Before long she was back on the wine and cheese circuit where at one event she met a rare book dealer with whom she exchanged cards, the man presently sitting across from her. She met him again, and again, and ended up marrying him with her uncle's blessing. They were now three to a house, soon to be four, when the baby arrived.

Billie set the letter aside and walked to a desk to retrieve a road atlas. She checked again for Woodland Hills.

No such place, according to the map.

She knew better. It had a name. It had a history. Someday, she would make it back that way, if only to track down Mr. Stark to hear his story.

On second thought, maybe not.

What's coming from

Echelon Press

Echelon Press

Summer 2004

From

Echelon Edge

See Fox Run

By

Lorna Schultz Nicholson

PROLOGUE

She looks around her small room, her last home on earth. Silently, slowly, her dark stony eyes stare at every corner, every crevice, every rough bump on the painted blocks of concrete. Drums beat to her ears alone, reminding her of pleasant childhood memories. She smiles. She is going there, going home; it's been too long.

The drums, made of caribou hide and birch, grow louder, beckoning her, drawing her into their soul. She turns her head, almost to the rhythm of their beat, to stare at the sink, the toilet bowl, the walls, the shelves. There are no photographs anywhere; no crayon scribbles, no past lovers, no smiling children who once nestled quietly in the comfort of her womb. The vision of her oldest boy, now a teenager, his eyes searching, longing, skips through her mind. But as quickly as he appears, he disappears, like a sputtering, fading flashbulb.

Her room is empty; she is empty.

She looks down at her hand. It holds a whalebone carving of a mother carrying a smiling baby in a papoose on her back. She squeezes her fist until the veins running haphazardly across her wrist look like turquoise ribbons. In her other hand, she holds the sharp end of the razor she has kept hidden until today.

Pressing it to her veins, she draws blood. Just a drop. A trickle. She stares at the blood, licks it, then licks the tip of the carving to spread her blood to the baby's face. The carving used to hang from her neck by a moose leather strap but that strap was not allowed once these walls became her home.

Strap or no strap, today she feels lucky. She is going to her real home.

She repeatedly touches her wrist with the razor, digging the sharpness into her skin, brazing the surface for it must go deeper–into the depth of the blue. Blood spurts, and she continues to slice.

She wants to go where the land in winter is an enormous eternity of whiteness and the sky in summer shines a forever light. Either season, there is whiteness. And belonging. It also means drumming, dancing in parkas, sharing fish and caribou with people her soul can touch. She sees beloved faces long gone, her *amaamak* and *aapak*.

In her mind, she searches for the whiteness, stretches her arms to reach it, touch it, embrace it. But all she sees is the red blood dripping from her wrists. She probes the razor deeper.

Yarayuami; I am tired, she cries.

Qiqirurnigaa; it has become cold, she moans.

The drum beat fades.

ONE

Why couldn't he think of a title for his sermon Sunday?

Intuko rubbed his temples, reclined in his brown leather chair that was cracking from wear, and planted his feet on the floor. He tapped his pen on the arm of the chair, then leaned forward and jotted down a few words. As he stared at the words, he shook his head. No good. He scratched them out. Frustrated, he closed his eyes.

Every Thursday he encountered the same dilemma, thinking of the appropriate heading for Sunday's sermon to put in the bulletins. Most members in his struggling downtown Vancouver church seemed to accept the fact that there was often an empty space beside the word *sermon* in Sunday's bulletin. Intuko had joked about it, asking everyone to bear with him; the title always came to him on Friday–a day too late. He'd even spent a Sunday preaching about *Fumbling Towards Ecstasy*, and used this as an example. Of course, the idea also came from the fact that *Fumbling Towards Ecstasy* was the title of Sarah McLachlan's CD, which he listened to a great deal.

A knock rattled his office door and when he opened his eyes he saw Hazel peeking around the corner.

"Intuko?"

"Hazel, come on in."

"It's Thursday. The bulletin needs—"

"I know."

Hazel chuckled and stepped into his office. "Don't forget," she said jokingly, wagging her finger at him, "we should look at our failures as gifts. That sermon of yours has stuck with me and helps me through some of *those* days. Don't be so hard on yourself."

Intuko smiled at the little woman, with short curly red hair and bright green eyes, standing by his office door. Hazel cheerfully fulfilled her job as secretary for Princess Street United Church, always staying on top of what needed to be done. With the church's financial woes, the job was only part-time but she'd already raised her daughter single-handedly and was now a doting grandmother.

Hazel walked proudly and officiously, in her soft-soled Wallabies, toward Intuko's desk.

"I have some messages for you. I didn't want to disturb you earlier." She clutched a handful of pink message slips in her hand. "Let's see, Joe at Street People Ministry rang."

"Did he say what he wanted?" Intuko stuck his pen behind his ear.

"I think he wants you to help out with the teens on Wednesday night. I guess they've got so many homeless kids coming to the street bus that they're overwhelmed."

"That's a good thing. I'll call him back. He's doing a great job with SPM."

"Do you miss being at the helm?" She slid him the message slip.

"That's a tough question Hazel. It's such an emotional job. So many of our kids come for help but in the end they don't have the strength to follow through with the changes. You always hope for that one." He sighed. "What are my other messages?"

"Well, this was a strange one–talking about hoping for

that one–but Lola called."

"Lola!" Intuko immediately leaned forward and held out his hand for the message slip. "I haven't seen her in years." He glanced at the pink slip. "You're right, I always wanted her to straighten out and I thought she had it in her." Concerned, he looked up. "How did she sound?"

Hazel pursed her lips. "Not good." She paused for a split second before she said, "Intuko, I saw her the other day. Wearing next to nothing, and wiggling toward a car that had stopped. I'm sure it was her. She was around the corner from here, on Hastings and Main." She sadly shrugged her shoulders. "Such a shame. I liked that girl too."

Once again, Intuko glanced down at the pink paper. He turned it over to study the back. "She didn't leave a number? I'd like to call her."

"Sorry. I asked but she said she said she wouldn't have a phone for a few more days. *Jimmy* was getting her hooked up."

Intuko slumped in his chair and blew out a rush of air. "Her pimp, I take it?"

"That's my guess. It makes me sick that these guys prey on these young vulnerable women. Okay, the last message here is from a..." She stopped to read her own handwriting. "Susan Peterson, at the Women's Correctional Institute. I'm not sure what she wanted, she just said for you to ring her back."

Puzzled, Intuko reached for this last message slip. "This woman was at church last Sunday. When she introduced herself on the way out, she asked if I still taught Inuit art. I haven't taught in years so I have no idea how she tracked down my name. She wants me to teach a carving class at the prison where she works as an officer." He pulled his pen out from behind his ear and tapped it on his desk. "One day a week shouldn't take too much of my time."

"I still have the seal you carved for me out of that beautiful green stone." Hazel almost sang her words. "It sits on my mantel and I get more compliments on that than anything else in my house. This class would be good for you."

"You're right. It might be fun to get back to my art."

"And give you something to do besides work."

Intuko laughed. "Are you worrying about me again?"

"No," she said adamantly. "But you're a good artist and you shouldn't let all that talent be wasted. I always say art shows what's inside the true person. And your art is charming. Intuko, stop furrowing, your eyebrows are near touching one another. Now, could I get you a coffee?"

Intuko waved his arms to shoosh her away. "You're not here to fetch me coffee."

"I don't mind, really. Lordy-be, my old husband used to sit on his duff and wait. Sometimes, he'd wait a long time." She paused. "If there's nothing else, I do have to get back to my desk. We want to have *something* to hand out Sunday morning."

"You know the title will come to me tomorrow and…" His old friend stood with her hands clasped together and her head tilted to the side; a body position that indicated she had something else to say. "Hazel, what is it?"

"I don't mean to pry but this Susan woman, she wouldn't work at…that wouldn't be the same prison your mum ended up in?" Hazel's eyes widened. "Where she died, I mean?"

Meet the author:

Born and raised in Missouri at the doorstep of the Ozarks, Henry Hoffman is a former public library director and newspaper editor whose fiction and non-fiction works have appeared in a variety of literary and trade publications, including the *Midwesterner* and *Library Journal*. His first novel, *Bound,* a light mystery and romance, was published in 1990. It was followed by a novella, *An Enduring Evil,* a dark tale of mental illness and threatened familial relationships, published in 2001. Along with his works of fiction, he has contributed articles to a number of standard reference works, including the *Encyclopedia of Library and Information Science and* the *Encyclopedia of Natural Disasters.* He currently resides in Southwest Florida.

Printed in the United States
29024LVS00001B/162

9 781590 803080